SHORT STORIES

THE PEARL

The Pearl

Throughout the darks and lights, throughout the grays, it rules the darkness. That orb in the sky rules our lives. It is the precious pearl, God's island in the sky.

Tonight in this black and white world, the moon showed a luster as moonlight beamed softly, lighting the recently rained-upon streets. A taxi meandered down the road and came to a stop. The lamp light competed with the moon. Standing in the darkness was a man in a black trench coat with a goatee. Out of the taxi emerged a man in a black fedora hat. The two men met. They walked into an alley. The man in the fedora was carrying a large satchel. The man in the black trench coat pulled on his goatee and said, "Did you get it?"

The man in the fedora held up the satchel. "It was hard to come by, Dr. Faustus. This one will cost you."

Dr. Faustus smiled. "Whatever the cost, it is always worth it." Faustus pulled an envelope from his trench coat pocket. He opened the envelope. "It is as you requested, and a lot better. The contract is a thousand years of bliss."

The man with the fedora looked at the paper. "A thousand years of bliss buys a lot of cans of tuna." The two men laughed.

Then the man in the fedora stuck his hand in the satchel. He pulled out a giant pearl, spotless and glowing with mysterious light. Suddenly the two men could hear a lion roaring in the distance. Dr. Faustus looked up. "You sure you weren't followed?"

The man in the fedora turned. "Damn. I was careless."

Dr. Faustus took the satchel and pearl and walked over to the taxi. "You have your payment. So long."

The man in the fedora ran for the taxi, but Dr. Faustus closed and locked the door. "Step on it," Dr. Faustus said to the cab driver.

The man in the fedora heard a growl and turned to look. A lion leapt through the air and grabbed him by the neck. The wind carried off the payment in the envelope. Another lion chased the cab, but it got away. Ten lions wandered the streets where the meeting had taken place.

* * *

Daisy woke first, her short, blond hair framing her face. Tamara, her sister, awoke a few minutes later. Tamara was four years older; Daisy was only six. Tamara's wild mane of red hair was in her face as she said, "The lions were so real."

Daisy looked at her sister. "Yes, you could almost touch their fur."

Tamara shook her head. "How did you see the lions? They were in my dream."

Daisy shook her head. "No. The lions were in my dream."

Tamara brushed her tangled hair. "If you saw the lions, then you saw the man in the black trench coat steal the pearl."

"Yes, the lions were after him, and they killed the man with the hat."

They both broke out in laughter. Daisy jumped on Tamara's bed. The sisters hugged. Tamara said. "We had the same dream. But how do people have the same dream?"

Daisy looked at her sister. "Maybe it's genetic? We are sisters, after all."

Tamara thought for a moment. "Something else is happening. When we dream tonight, we will find out."

With that, Tamara and Daisy went to breakfast.

They got dressed and went to school. They played and studied. Then it was night again and time to go to sleep. Daisy went to kiss her father good night. "Daddy," she asked, "can two people dream the same dream?"

Her father thought for a moment. "I guess so. But it would be an act of profound synchronicity."

Daisy nodded. "What is synchronicity?"

Her father kissed her. "It's like when we think the same thought or when we do something at the same time as someone else."

"Like a dream?"

"Yes, like a dream."

Tamara then approached and kissed her father good night. The girls left hand in hand to go to bed. They swiftly went to sleep. Suddenly everything was black, white, and gray. Tamara turned to see Daisy. "I can see you," said Tamara.

Daisy smiled. "I can see you too."

"Are we dreaming or awake?" asked Tamara.

A man's voice interrupted the sisters. "You are dreaming." He was tall and wore a leather jacket and a baseball cap with a lion emblem on it.

"Who are you?" asked Tamara.

The man smiled and extended his hand. "I'm Gavin. I'm here to help."

Daisy looked around. "This must be a dream because when I'm awake, it is in color."

Gavin looked down at Daisy. "It's like that so you know the difference between dreaming and awake."

Tamara looked at her sister. "Why are Daisy and I sharing the same dream?"

4

Gavin looked at Tamara. "So you can help each other."

Daisy walked up to Gavin. "Are we in trouble?"

Gavin waved. "Come with me and I'll explain." They walked a bit and an airport appeared. "You remember last night's dream?"

Tamara looked out as an airplane took off. "The man in the black trench coat stole the pearl."

"Yes, that is right, and the pearl is very important, especially to you." A biplane taxied down the runway. On its side was the emblem of a lion with the words *Roaring Angels* written beneath.

Daisy looked at Gavin. "Are you an angel?"

Gavin smiled. "I am a pilot, and in that way, a guide on your journey."

Tamara turned to Gavin. "What is the pearl?"

Gavin smiled. "Pearl, delighting a prince's pleasure, chastely imprisoned in purest gold! There never came a costlier treasure from all the east, I firmly hold; so fine, so smooth on every side. So round, so radiant, however set, that I gave this pearl the place of pride above all jewels I judged as yet. Alas! In a garden I lost it, let it go to the ground on a grassy plot. Bereft of love, I am racked by regret for my pearl, my own pearl without a spot."

Tamara thought a moment. "We lost the pearl. That man took it away. But what is it?"

Daisy smiled. "He stole our joy."

Gavin smiled. "Close, but not yet right. The poem I recited was 'The Pearl,' a medieval poem. Understand the poem and you will know what the pearl is. I can't help you any further. It is important that you discover some things for yourselves."

Tamara and Daisy awoke the next morning, a Saturday. Their mother made them breakfast and asked them what they wanted for Christmas, for that season was already upon them. The girls said they would write to Santa Claus, and off they went to the computer. There Tamara looked up the medieval poem "The Pearl." They printed it and began to read it. After a while, their father looked over their shoulders. "What are you reading there, girls? 'The Pearl,' I remember it. I read it in college in my English lit class. It's an allegory."

Daisy looked up at her father. "What is an allegory?"

"It's a literary device in which an object symbolizes a religious principle, in this case."

Tamara looked up at her father. "We have been reading it for an hour and we still don't know what the pearl is."

Their father looked at the poem. "I never understood it myself. I think you should read this when you are older. You will have so much more to bring to it." Their father let the girls continue to read and analyze the poem.

Daisy said, "I think the pearl is the lady. He calls her his pearl."

Tamara shook her head. "The pearl is the City of God. It's what the poet can't reach without submitting wholly to God's will." Suddenly the wind flashed through the house, blowing the poem across the room. There the last page sat at the top. And it read, "So pearl to God I dedicated, with Christ's blessing and with mine. May he who in form of bread and wine the priest shows daily, grant we find ourselves true servants to him divine, and precious pearls to please his mind."

Tamara stared at the page. "What pearl do we all have in common, that we love more than the purest lady and that for lack of it we can not go into the City of God?"

Daisy smiled. "God wants souls."

Tamara hugged her sister. "The pearl is the soul."

The sisters prayed before they went to bed. "Now I lay me down to sleep, I pray the Lord my soul to keep. May God guard me through the night and wake me in the morning light. Amen." With that, Daisy and Tamara hugged and went straight to sleep.

They entered their dream, where it was raining and storming. Gavin met them. His leather bomber jacket was stained dark by the rain. He said, "Come, let me take you to where I live." He hailed a taxi. They entered and Gavin told the driver, "Take us to paradise." The taxi meandered down the gray tones of the city streets. Gavin looked at the girls. "By now you know that pearls are spotless souls. They are souls without sin, usually the souls of children or saints. Look out the window." Tamara and Daisy looked out the taxi window. There they saw a river, and in the river there were floating paper lanterns going downstream. Gavin pointed at the lanterns. "Those lanterns are pearls. They shine with the light of God. They go downstream toward the City of God. That city is lit by the souls of the pure. God, the purest soul, is the brightest light in the city. We all start our path on the river that leads to the City of God. But life leads us astray and our pearl loses light and takes a different path. Few make it to the City of God. "

Daisy looked up at Gavin. "Where do the pearls come from?"

Gavin smiled. "They come from the Lady of the Pearls. She is the bounty of life. Before you are born, a grain of sand that is your yet-unmade soul is deposited with the lady. The grain of sand holds your past lives, if you have had any, and it will be turned into a pearl through the lady's love."

The taxi came to a stop. There was a neon sign that read *PAIR-A-DICE CASINO AND AIRFIELD*. The neon dice changed back and forth from snake eyes to a seven. They exited the taxi and entered the casino. There at the entrance of the casino was a man in a white dinner jacket and black bow tie. Gavin introduced the man. "This is Hap. He runs the casino."

Hap smiled at the girls. "Would you like to test your ability at the tables?" Tamara looked toward the tables.

"The house always wins," Hap laughed. "That is the point."

Tamara swept a red lock from her forehead. "If I can not win, than it's best not to play."

Hap took out a gold cigarette case. "Sometimes you must take a chance."

Tamara looked at Hap. "Even if you lose?"

Hap took out a gold-tipped cigarette. "Sometimes you win." Hap lit his cigarette. "You don't have to play, but you do have to meet the rest of the gang."

Gavin smiled. "Come with me."

They went to the hangar. A DC-3 and a biplane were parked in the hangar. The DC-3 had *Roaring Angel*

Airlines written on the side with the logo of a lion. Driving a luggage carrier came two men in lion baseball caps. They waved at Gavin and the girls. One jumped out and went to meet the girls. He shook each girl's hand. Gavin introduced him as Jedidiah. "I'm a logistics specialist," he said.

The other man stopped the luggage cart and went over to meet the girls. He spat his chewing tobacco and said, "Don't listen to him; we are the cargo guys. They call me Spit."

Just then, a biplane came speeding up to the hangar. The pilot waved. Gavin said, "That's Chuck, one of the other pilots." The girls waved at Chuck.

A man in a waistcoat met them in the hangar. "Hi, I'm Burt. I'm the casino waiter. Will they be staying for supper?" Gavin nodded.

Two men walked out of the hangar office. Sitting near the office was another man cleaning a shotgun. Gavin and the girls walked up to him. Gavin smiled. "This is Skeet, another one of my fellow pilots."

A man in a white shirt grinned. "They may be pilots, but they go nowhere without us. My name is Flo. And this is Brain."

The second man, also in a white shirt, had a slide rule in his pocket. "We are the air traffic controllers."

Gavin smiled. "They are the tower guys."

Gavin and the girls walked close to the DC-3. A man in the cockpit waved. Gavin laughed. "That's Money, the last of the four pilots."

Coming down the DC-3 stairs was the most beautiful flight attendant the girls had ever seen. She had a lovely pearl necklace. She hugged the girls. "My name is Alphaea."

Daisy tugged at Gavin's pant leg. "Is she your girlfriend?"

Gavin laughed. "No, she's Z's girlfriend."

Tamara looked at Gavin. "Who's Z?"

Just then, a man covered in grease came from inside the DC-3. He hugged Alphaea and met the kids. "I'm Z. I'm the mechanic. I'm the guy that makes everything work."

Gavin smiled. "He's more than that; he and Alphaea own Pair-a-Dice. They are the co-owners."

Z turned to Gavin. "Have you told them yet?" Gavin shook his head.

Tamara looked up at Gavin. "Told us what?"

Z looked at Alphaea, then at the children. "What Gavin has not told you is that Tamara's pearl was stolen and that by midnight, she must join the pearl in Dr. Faustus factory."

Tamara and Daisy looked at each other. Daisy said, "What will we do?"

Gavin looked at the children. "There is nothing to do. It is the way it is. You will join us for supper, then we will take you to the factory."

Tears were in the girls' eyes. Z turned to the girls. "Everything that must be done must come from you, not from us."

Alphaea hugged the children. "It is you, your character, your resolve, that will see you through. We have faith in you and we love you very much."

Burt walked up. "Children, supper is served."

Tamara looked at Burt. "I don't think I'm very hungry."

Burt smiled. "You have a lot ahead of you; it is wise to eat well. You will need your strength."

* * *

When they were done, it was time to go. Alphaea held Daisy in her arms. "When the time comes, Daisy, you will have to let your sister go alone. You must not enter Dr. Faustus's factory. Dr. Faustus must not have two souls for the price of one."

Daisy looked up at Alphaea. "Then how do I help Tamara?"

Alphaea stroked Daisy's golden hair. "You will find a way to help, but not in the factory. Only Tamara may go into the factory."

Gavin put the girls in a cab. The cab driver smiled. Gavin got in next to the girls and the cab sped off. All the Roaring Angels waved from the casino entrance.

The rain poured as they drove, punctuated by flashes of lightning. Through the rain, they could see the pearl lanterns floating downstream.

Tamara asked, "Am I going to hell?"

Gavin stroked her hair. "There is no hell. Dr. Faustus was once a pearl on the stream to the City of God. He lost his way so badly that his pearl lost all light. He needs perfect pearls like yours to have enough light to exist. Once he loses his light, his candle will be extinguished forever."

Daisy hugged Gavin. "Why don't you stop Dr. Faustus if he is breaking the law?"

Gavin smiled. "Dr. Faustus is doing wrong, but he is not breaking our laws. We cannot interfere with souls that do wrong. He knows what is right, and when he chooses to do it, then we can guide him closer to the light."

Tamara clasped her hands together. "So he has a good side?"

Gavin looked at Tamara. "All creatures are inherently good, and we love all of them. It is just that they lose their way."

The cab came to a stop before the factory gate. Dr. Faustus was waiting at the entrance with a guard. Tamara kissed Daisy. Daisy hugged her back. Gavin opened the door to the cab. Tamara walked toward Dr. Faustus. Gavin called out, "Tamara, remember, hope in the darkness is all we have. Nothing is inevitable. Believe in your destiny and it will come true."

Dr. Faustus interrupted, "Until you find a destiny, your soul is mine. Never forget that." With that, Dr. Faustus and the guard walked Tamara into the factory.

Once inside the factory, they walked to Dr. Faustus's office. There the doctor pointed at a contract on his desk. "It will make your stay much easier if you sign this agreement now."

Tamara looked at the contract. "I don't think I want to sign this. It gives you sole possession of my soul."

Dr. Faustus laughed. "I already have possession of your pearl, so you have no way to escape. I am just being kind. In exchange for giving me your soul willingly, I will give you special and kind treatment."

Tamara brushed the contract off the desk with her hand. "I will not sign this, not now, not ever!"

Anger flushed Dr. Faustus's face. "Young lady, you will sign this contract. It is only a matter of time."

With that, the guards dragged Tamara away.

Tamara was given factory overalls, a bucket, and a brush. She was commanded to wash all the floors in the enormous factory until she relented and signed the contract. But Tamara would not relent; she would never give up, not if it took all eternity.

Dr. Faustus said, "It may take all eternity, but I have plenty of time. You suffer needlessly for something you no longer own."

* * *

Daisy woke up from her dream and saw Tamara still sleeping. She shook her sister, but Tamara did not wake up.

Daisy ran into her parents' room screaming, "You have to help Tamara! Dr. Faustus has her in the factory."

Her mother got up and said, "Daisy, you're having a nightmare. Let me tuck you back into bed." Her mother carried Daisy back into her bedroom. "See, Tamara is all right. She's sleeping soundly."

Daisy began crying. "Tamara won't wake up!"

Her mother sighed and shook Tamara, who still didn't wake up. Her mother checked her forehead. "She's burning up!"

An ambulance came and took Tamara away to the hospital. Their father drove Daisy and her mother to the hospital.

Daisy said, "Is Tamara going to live?"

Her father said, "Of course, Daisy, but she is very sick."

They arrived at the hospital and went to Tamara's room. Her father and mother talked to the doctors as Daisy sat next to her unconscious sister and held her hand. Soon Daisy was asleep.

* * *

Gavin smiled. "Welcome back, Daisy."

Daisy looked up and saw Gavin standing next to a Roaring Angel biplane. Daisy walked to his side. She said, "Take me to God."

Gavin took her by the hand. "I thought you might say that."

Daisy looked up at Gavin. "Is it possible to see God?"

Gavin nodded. "It is. But you must have a relative speak for you. This relative must be already in the City of God."

Daisy sighed. "I don't know if I already have a relative in the City of God."

Gavin smiled. "I'll take you there and we'll find out."

The Roaring Angel biplane took to the sky, Gavin in the front seat flying the plane and Daisy in the back seat. The aircraft followed the stream of lanterns that led to the City of God. Daisy could see that the pearl lanterns did not all follow the same stream. Some turned into tributaries that eventually led back to the main stream, while others followed tributaries that led farther and farther away from the City of God.

The biplane banked as the streams met a mountain range. Here the stream became singular as all tributaries no longer could lead back due to the mountains interposing themselves. The aircraft went into a canyon flying sideways. It was becoming dark; they could see the pearl lanterns dotting the dusk with their lights. As the biplane entered the dark mouth of the gorge, they could see an enormous bright light in the distance. The bright light got bigger and bigger until the aircraft exited the canyon; suddenly Daisy saw a metropolis lighting the night sky.

Gavin got on the radio and said, "City of God, this is Roaring Angel One, requesting permission to land at the visitors' field outside the city gates."

They heard static over the radio for a moment. "Roaring Angel One, proceed to the visitors' field, permission granted."

The biplane flew over the city. Daisy could see beautiful buildings and canals that cut across the city in concentric circles. At the center of the city was an enormous skyscraper that blazed with a light that was so bright it overwhelmed all the other lights. Daisy could also see millions of pearl lanterns dotting the canals of the city.

The biplane landed on an airfield lit with flares that lay outside the city walls. The aircraft came to a stop and Gavin undid Daisy's seatbelt. Soon they were walking toward the city.

Gavin said to Daisy, "We can only go as far as Centerbridge, the gate of the city. There someone must speak for you or we will have to go back."

They approached Centerbridge; underneath the bridge, they could see glowing pearl lanterns entering the City of God. At the center of the bridge was a gate with a guard in a lion baseball cap. Gavin nodded at the guard and they greeted one another by name.

The guard looked at Daisy. "Who do we have here?"

Gavin smiled. "This is Daisy. She has come to see if anyone in the city will speak for her."

The guard looked toward the city. "You are awfully young to know someone in this city."

Daisy looked up at both of them. "How do we do this? How do we find out?"

There was a large light at the gate itself. The guard pointed at it. "Touch that light and anyone you know here will speak for you."

"What does speak for me mean?"

Gavin said, "They will vouch for you, and through their guidance alone will you see God."

Daisy looked up at Gavin. "Does that mean you will not be with me?"

Gavin smiled. "No, I will be with you every step if you like."

"Thank you," said Daisy. Then she walked toward the light. She looked back at Gavin once she was only a step away. "Will it hurt?"

The guard grinned. "It may feel funny, but it won't hurt you."

Daisy brought her hand closer and closer to the light. She thought about how terrible it must be for Tamara. She sighed and put her hand into the light. "It tickles," said Daisy. "How long do I have to keep my hand in?"

Gavin looked at the guard. "You can take it out already."

Daisy rubbed her hand. "How will I know if it worked?"

The guard walked forward. "Someone will come to the gate and claim you."

They waited for a few minutes. The guard said, "Usually they show up immediately." They waited for an hour and still nobody showed up to claim Daisy. The guard said, "I'm sorry, I don't think anyone will come and speak for you. You are just too young to know anyone here."

Gavin looked at his watch. "It's time to go, Daisy."

Daisy grabbed Gavin's hand. "But I want to see God."

Gavin closed his eyes. "Maybe not today, Daisy, but someday."

Daisy tugged on Gavin's hand. "But how will we save Tamara?"

Gavin looked into Daisy's eyes and said. "We will have to find another way."

Just as they were leaving, the guard screamed, "Wait! The gate is opening!"

Daisy looked up at Gavin. "What does that mean?"

Gavin smiled. "It means someone is speaking for you and you will be admitted to see God."

At the gate was a woman standing in a white robe. Daisy and Gavin met her. She smiled a beatific smile. "I am your Aunt Martha. You never knew me; I died before you were born. I'm sorry it took so long to claim you. We had to change our protocols to admit you, and that took no small doing. The problem was that you don't actually know me. But I have been watching you from birth. We had to decide whether that was enough."

Daisy hugged Aunt Martha. "Thank you. But could

not God just make the decision? He is all powerful, isn't he?"

Aunt Martha smiled as she looked at Gavin. "It's a democracy here, darling. God decides with us, not above us. It's like a constitutional monarchy, but the king here, God, has equal power with the council of angels. Neither can effect action without the other."

Gavin looked at his watch. "We need to get this done before Dr. Faustus convinces Tamara to sign his contract. Then it will be too late."

* * *

Back at Dr. Faustus's factory, Tamara was still washing the floors with a brush and a bucket. Dr. Faustus appeared with a juicy hamburger in his hand. "After a full day of working, I'm sure you're hungry."

Tamara looked up at the delicious hamburger. "Yes, I'm so hungry, I could faint."

Dr. Faustus offered Tamara the burger. Just as she was reaching for it, he pulled it away. "First you must sign the contract."

Tamara sighed. "I will never sign that contract. Not ever."

Dr. Faustus said, "Suit yourself." He took a big bite out of the hamburger. "It's a shame—this is the best hamburger I've ever tasted."

Meanwhile, Daisy, Martha, and Gavin walked through the City of God. People waved but did not stop to talk. They reached a round, tall building that sandwiched the skyscraper of God on all sides. Martha said, "This is the Council of Angels. We must go through it to reach God's palace." They walked through the building. On all sides, there were statues of lions and winged angels.

They soon reached God's palace, where they saw a large statue of a winged lion surrounded by pearls. The winged lion had a pearl where his third eye lay. Daisy said, "Is that what God looks like?"

Gavin smiled. "It is an impression of God. You will see the real God shortly."

Martha showed them into a room that led to elevators. Martha said, "This is the announcement room. Here they will announce you to God."

A man in a suit and a clipboard walked up to them. "Is God expecting you?"

Martha met him. "Yes, God expects us. I am Martha. This is the child whom I have spoken for and this is the angel Gavin."

The man in the suit looked down at the clipboard. "And the child is named?"

Martha said. "Daisy."

The man in the suit underlined something with his pen. "God is indeed expecting you. Pass on through and take elevator one."

They walked through and saw that all elevators were numbered one. It was a way of saying that here, all elevators led to God. They pressed the button on the first elevator they found. They entered when it opened. And the doors closed behind them.

Martha spoke. "I must tell you, child, that God is irascible and frightening and has a quite a temper."

Gavin smiled. "Whatever you see, do not be afraid."

The elevator sped to the top with great speed. As

they reached the top, through the elevator window they could see clouds. The door opened and they walked into God's palace. It was all gold and diamonds and pearls. There in the center of the room was a dark cloud that emanated white light.

Daisy looked at the stormy cloud. "Is that God?" Gavin and Martha both nodded in the affirmative.

The cloud spoke with a deep, resounding voice. "Daisy, what do you want from your God?"

Gavin spoke to Daisy. "This is your chance. Speak to God. Don't be afraid."

Daisy walked up to the cloud. "My sister Tamara has had her pearl stolen by Dr. Faustus."

"You come here for selfish reasons!" A sudden wind picked up in the room and pushed against Daisy.

"It is for my sister, not for me!" said Daisy.

"In your soul, you think you need your sister, so it is selfish, not selfless," said God.

Then Daisy began to cry. "You are mean!"

Then the cloud roared like a lion. "I am God!"

Daisy turned around and headed for the elevator door. "He won't help. He is mean. We are wasting our time here!"

Then the wind picked up and a wild thunderstorm ensued. "Wait!" said God. When the storm subsided, a man stood where the cloud had once stormed.

Daisy looked at the man and recognized his face. She yelled and ran forward toward him. "Z!" Z hugged Daisy tightly.

Meanwhile, at the factory, Tamara continued to wash the floors. She was exhausted. Then a chocolate sundae appeared in front of her. "Taste and you shall be free," a voice said. Tamara reached for the spoon. As she did so, the spoon became a pen and the sundae transformed into a contract. Tamara was about to cry, but she held back her tears.

Dr. Faustus leaned over kindly. "You need not suffer. It's just a signature, nothing big. Sign and you will be eating sundaes at every meal."

Tamara was trembling with exhaustion, but she threw the contract in the doctor's face. "Never means never."

Dr. Faustus laughed. "You will sign eventually. They all sign. It's the way of the world. It just means I must try harder to convince you." He rolled up the contract. "You need to get a harder job. One on the factory floor fixing razors to razor blades. That will change your mind for certain."

Back in the City of God, Z smiled. "We can help you, but there will be risk at every turn."

Daisy hugged Z. "I will do anything it takes."

Z stroked Daisy's hair. "We will rescue your sister, but in the process, we will rescue all souls under the control of Dr. Faustus. You must promise me you will work so that this is a selfless act made only to release all those souls from bondage. "

Daisy smiled. "I will be selfless, Z."

"Even if you lose your sister?"

Daisy gulped. "Yes, even if I lose Tamara."

Z walked over to two red doors. "Then you must go to the Lady of Pearls and ask for possession of your pearl."

Gavin cradled Daisy's head against his hand. "This is the first step, Daisy."

Martha smiled. "We love you. Always remember that."

Z walked Daisy to the two red doors. "One of these doors leads to the Lady of Pearls and the other leads to the lion. Choose the right door and you will not only live, but also be able to save your sister. Choose the wrong door and you will surely perish and nobody will help your sister forevermore."

Daisy looked at the doors. They both looked exactly the same. "I can't choose; they are identical. What do I do?"

Gavin said, "Feel which one is the right one."

Martha spoke. "Have faith child."

Daisy looked at Z, then at the doors. She remembered that all elevators lead to God, so all doors must lead to the lady. Under her breath, Daisy said. "That's what I feel." She opened a red door. "Life is an act of faith."

Z smiled. "You opened the right door, Daisy. Now go in and see the Lady of the Pearls."

"Do I have to go alone?"

Z held the door open. "Of coarse they can go with you."

Daisy, Martha, and Gavin entered the door's threshold and disappeared.

Meanwhile, Tamara was putting razor blades on a razor on a conveyer belt. A guard with a whip said, "Faster!" striking Tamara with the whip. Tamara cut her fingers as she tried to put the razors on faster. Her hands were a bloody mess.

Dr. Faustus appeared with hydrogen peroxide in a black bottle. He put it on her hands and she screamed with pain. "No Band-Aids," said the doctor. "This can all stop if you will sign the contract. Otherwise, there won't be much left of your hands."

Tamara looked at her bloody hands. "I will never sign your contract, not even if you cut my hands off!"

Dr. Faustus looked at Tamara angrily. "For that you will clean toilets with a toothbrush."

Tamara rubbed her hands together. "I'll infect my hands."

The doctor laughed. "That is precisely what will happen, and I will no longer give you hydrogen peroxide. You will sign my contract. Your will is not greater than mine. I have done this for a very long time. I have broken much stronger people than you."

Meanwhile, Daisy and Martha followed Gavin, who walked up ahead on a trail in a forest. The moon was full, so they could all see well. Daisy said, "How far is it, Gavin?"

Gavin looked at his watch. "Can't you hear the ocean? It's just ahead."

Daisy turned to Martha. "So you've never been here before?"

Martha smiled. "I've met the Lady of the Pearls, but only in the city, not here. Most of the inhabitants of the city have never been here. This is where the pearls come from. She is the mother of life. Pearls for trees and hawks and panthers, all the souls of everything come from her."

They began to walk on a beach. The tide was low. Just ahead, they could see a cave carved by the sea into the cliff stone that reached up toward the sky. Standing in a gauzy dress in the surf was a beautiful woman, long and graceful as a ballerina. She turned and looked at them. As she turned, Daisy recognized her face.

Daisy came running down the beach and into the surf. "Alphaea!" Daisy jumped up in her arms and Alphaea held her close and kissed her forehead.

Daisy said, "You are the Lady of Pearls."

"Yes, I am, sweetness," said Alphaea. "You want to gain access to your pearl? As you are no older than six, your pearl still remains in my possession. If you were a little older, like Tamara, then I would have already set you to follow the stream. I will take you to your pearl, but you must retrieve it yourself because I cannot touch it. Only you can."

Alphaea carried Daisy in her arms and walked up the beach as Gavin and Martha followed. She soon came to a boat shaped like a swan. Gavin and Martha helped push the boat into the water and Alphaea put Daisy down. Alphaea fixed the sails and with a hand gesture, the wind began to billow the cloth, causing the boat to move forward.

As Alphaea sailed the boat, the moon reflected off the waves. They soon arrived at a spot that Alphaea seemed to know. She said, "From the grain of spirit, sometimes new, sometimes old, I make each soul into a perfect, spotless pearl. Some lose their shine in time. Others never do, and those that never do make it to the City of God. It is how it has always been and will always be. Making a pearl takes time, but it can lose its shine in a foolish instant. I only make the pearls, but God must guide them to the light. You must listen to all your angels if you are to make it one day to the city."

Alphaea waved her hand over Daisy. Suddenly the

ocean frothed with bubbles. A clamshell burst through the surface and floated on the water.

Alphaea took a necklace off her neck and put it on Daisy. The necklace had many multicolored pearls, but the two biggest white pearls, fused together, shone in the moonlight. "This is the necklace of our union. Just like you have a pearl, I have a pearl, and Z has a pearl as well. The love between Z and I is the union of two spirits that make one. It is our eternal marriage, and together our union makes one universe. We are opposites that attract and make a single spirit. Like stars within stars, we are the bow of infinity and our love begets the flower of galaxies as well as all life extant in the cosmos."

Daisy looked at the necklace. Alphaea looked at Daisy with great seriousness. "This necklace will allow you to walk on water to retrieve your pearl, but only if you are undertaking a selfless act. Otherwise, it will drag you under the waves and you will drown."

Alphaea swept locks of hair off Daisy's face. "You don't have to do this."

Daisy gulped. "I have come so far, I can't turn back now."

Martha turned to Daisy. "Think of Tamara, but believe you are saving all beings by saving her. The universe is present in all of us. Think of the universe in her eyes."

Daisy nodded. She climbed over the side of the boat. She planted her foot firmly on the water's surface. Then she brought her second foot down and it sank beneath the water. She began to sink and thrash in the water. Gavin caught her hand and pulled her up out of the water. "Thank you," said Daisy.

Gavin held her in his arms. "We will find another way. You don't have to do this. You are conflicted and you will drown."

Daisy took in a deep breath and released it. "I can do it!! Put me down on the waves."

Daisy suddenly thought of the many people who had tried to help her. Now she would return the favor and save them. The water was solid and Daisy walked on it as if on a rough stone path. She took each step carefully and soon was at the clamshell.

The pearl shined brightly. She thought it is so beautiful. So many need their pearls returned, she thought, and by my courage, by my selfless act, I will make it so. She picked up the pearl and returned to the boat. Alphaea hugged Daisy and the pearl close. "By your selfless act, millions will be redeemed. Bless you, Daisy."

Gavin spoke. "Now we can do what needs to be done and in the process, save your Tamara." Daisy was not sure she knew what they were talking about, but she knew she was on the cusp of saving her sister.

* * *

Tamara was cleaning toilets with a toothbrush. Her hands were infected and covered with sores. She was so tired and hungry that she could hardly move anymore. She stared down the mouth of a toilet and began to fall asleep. Then suddenly, Dr. Faustus appeared and said, "No sleeping. No rest for the wicked."

Tamara almost began to cry. "I'm so tired and

hungry, but if I could just sleep for a little while. . . ." The doctor shook his head. "No contract, no sleep." He unfurled the contract in front of her.

Tamara sleepily picked up the pen and was about to sign when suddenly she woke herself up with a scream. "Never!"

The doctor shook his head. "I have been trying to spare you the worst. Take her to the laboratory. You shall be our guinea pig. We will test all our new products on you. It shall be very painful. You will wish you could die, but you can't die here, and that means inexhaustible torture until you give in."

Tamara saw that she could not win, that she had been abandoned to become a lost soul. She grabbed the contract and began signing her name. Dr. Faustus smiled.

Suddenly, there was a commotion and lions could be heard roaring. Tamara dropped the contract. The wall came crashing down in front of them like it was made out of paper. A lion walked forward with Daisy on its back holding her pearl.

Dr. Faustus cringed in a corner.

Tamara walked up to her sister. "What took you so long?"

Daisy stayed on the lions' back. "We figured out a way to save all the pearls, not just yours. But you never left my mind. I love you, sister."

Tamara rubbed the lion's side. "I love you, too."

The lost souls were all reunited with their pearls except Dr. Faustus, who no longer had a pearl of his own. Tamara held her pearl and it at once shone brightly. Dr. Faustus said, "My soul will be extinguished without those pearls. I am lost forever. Will nobody take pity on me?"

Gavin spoke from out of a lion's mouth. "You lost your pearl and there is nothing to be done. You have stolen the light of others, and there is no greater misdeed in this realm."

Dr. Faustus put his head down. "I feel oblivion coming."

Suddenly Tamara stepped forward. "Wait!" She offered her pearl to Dr. Faustus. "I will share my pearl with you."

The doctor looked into Tamara's eyes. "After all those things I did to you, you still forgive me?"

Dr. Faustus touched the pearl and it became twice as bright as before. Suddenly the pearl began to separate into two distinct pearls. Dr. Faustus took the new pearl with great joy. "My own pearl. I have never dreamed it could be so. Now I will care for it with the love of a new mother. Thank you. Thank you, you have redeemed me."

* * *

They all met one last time at the Pair-a-Dice Casino and Airfield. There everyone kissed and hugged the girls. Z and Alphaea threw a party. The girls were feted. When it was all over, they were told they would forget this dream. But they would always be close to their friends in their hearts.

Dr. Faustus turned the factory into a home for wayward souls. He would forevermore work to bring souls to the right path. Alphaea and Z would continue to rule the universe and the roaring angels would continue to watch over humanity.

Gavin said his good-byes and told the girls that he would watch over them for as long as it took for them to reach the City of God. They were on the stream, but their experience gave them an advantage. Gavin would have little to do but smile until they were reunited in heaven.

* * *

Tamara awoke to the full color of daylight. Her sister was next to her in the chair, also awake. The parents hugged their children. Soon they left the hospital and went home.

"What did you dream?" asked Daisy. "I can't remember."

"Neither can I," said Tamara.

On Christmas Day, there were jovial festivities. The girls unwrapped their Christmas gifts. Daisy opened a box with a fuzzy stuffed lion inside. She said, "I'll call it Gavin."

Then Tamara opened a small box and pulled out a pearl necklace with two large pearls fused together. "I'll look like a beautiful lady."

The dreams they had forgotten were written on their souls. The girls grew up to follow the guidance of their spirits. Martha and Gavin kept an eye on them. The stream to the City of God, which is lit by shining pearls, was changed forever by two courageous girls who believed in dreams.

SAINT OBERON

Saint Oberon

After spring came a sudden snow. It left the milkweed covered in crystals. The ice was cast over seven chrysalises. The sun began to thaw the plant. Drop after drop of water collected at the frail foot of the milkweed. Not a single cocoon stirred.

But inside one chrysalis something moved. It was Oberon, roused by the warm sunlight. It was dawn and the light glowed with the promise of birth. In an instant the chrysalis and ice cracked. Out slipped Oberon. His first thought was how warm the dawn. He looked at the six other pupae. They remained inert and lifeless. Oberon cried, as he knew that they would never bloom into butterflies.

Oberon slowly fluttered his wings and took flight. Dawn had just kissed the morning. He gained altitude and saw a butterfly chasing a bumblebee. He thought that looked like fun. Oberon began to chase the butterfly. It was a monarch like him, his mirror image, but female. Male monarchs have a black spot, whereas females do not.

The two butterflies frolicked through the forest. Deeper into the woods they went. The trees were tall and this made it dark at daylight. Oberon laughed and asked the butterfly her name. But she was coy until they were in the deepest part of the forest. Then she said, "I am Eugenia. You, Oberon, have been chosen. The spirit of the monarch butterfly flows through you. I will be your friend always."

"Wait!" cried Oberon. "Who are you?"

She simply said, "I am Eugenia, your friend."

He blinked and Eugenia was gone.

Oberon felt the migration in his veins. He met with other monarchs as he traveled north. But he did not see Eugenia. He asked if anybody had seen his friend.

"Eugenia?" they said. "Eugenia is dead. She died a very long time ago. If you look inside your soul you will know that she is the first monarch. She gave birth to us all."

Oberon sought out his soul and found Eugenia was there. For the rest of his life Oberon was left wondering who he had chased deep into the forest.

His life lingered for two months. Then, on the day before Oberon was to die, the sun shone enormously red and round. The rosy rays of light obscured his vision. Suddenly, like magic, she was there. Eugenia landed on a leaf next to Oberon.

She said, "You and the entire universe know that you will die tomorrow at dawn, but today is not to be wasted, for today is time to learn."

Oberon was very old; six weeks is a lifetime for monarch butterflies, and Oberon's body shook with age. "Why learn now before I die? How will I be able to use the information?"

Eugenia laughed. "Do you think I would teach you without purpose? I am, after all, Eugenia, the mother of all monarchs, and my appearance to you is no accident. I am a messenger from that being that you and all other creatures feel in their soul. Some call it God and others the universe. Your life holds special meaning."

Oberon looked at Eugenia. "But how will what I learn

cross the great darkness?"

Eugenia looked at Oberon with great compassion. "Believe what I tell you. Everything you learn today you will remember in the next life. It is only change, like when you were an egg and you became a caterpillar, and when you were a caterpillar you turned into a chrysalis, and when you were a chrysalis you changed into a butterfly. Change is all around you. You cannot help but change. Does not the moon change? Does not day turn to night? Does not each day turn different from the last? Nothing remains the same, and we must face change our whole lives. But you must not allow change to change you. You must remain steady. Like a great rock by the tempestuous sea, you must remain solid no matter how you are battered by change. Transience cannot be avoided; it is everywhere. You must flow with change and not fight against it."

Eugenia spoke until dusk and then she disappeared. In the darkness Oberon thought about what he had been told. *You can't let change change you. Death is nothing like passing through a mist. It is only change.* He suddenly realized the power of thinking that way. He did not look at the dawn with dread. *Change is what is normal,* he thought.

The sun rushed to rise over the horizon. The first rays rolled across the sky. Oberon sat tranquilly; it did not bother him that his life began to ebb from his body. It did not bother him that darkness began to swallow his being. *Change is inevitable; I will flow with it and be carried by its wind wheresoever it will take me.* In all the brightness of dawn, dark death claimed a butterfly.

Nearby, an egg sat dormant on milkweed. Inside was the reborn soul of Oberon. As an egg he would quickly hatch, then become a caterpillar. The milkweed was his food. It is poisonous to all but the monarch butterflies. Armed with that sustenance, monarchs are poisonous to all predators. Oberon ate the milkweed and remembered what Eugenia had told him in his previous life: change is natural; we must never be overwhelmed by it.

Oberon spun a cocoon around himself. To change from caterpillar to butterfly would take a small death. Every cell in Oberon's body would have to change. Oberon realized that once again it was time to die. Inside the cocoon Oberon turned to liquid and he was no longer a caterpillar. Oberon embraced the change and soon emerged from the chrysalis. He was a butterfly again, and even through his metamorphosis he remembered his past life and all that Eugenia had told him. Oberon joined the other monarch butterflies and headed north.

Monarchs listen to the heartbeat of the earth and go north to it. As Oberon was flying he noticed another butterfly near the tip of his wing. It was Eugenia and she asked him to follow her. They flew out of the wilderness and deeper and deeper into the city. Eugenia spoke. "What do you think the nature of suffering is?"

Oberon replied, "I don't know, I have never suffered."

Eugenia laughed. "How could you not suffer? Have you never been hungry? Have you never flown arduously against the wind?"

Oberon said, "I see what you mean. I actually have suffered, but mostly I am conscious of others' suffering."

Eugenia smiled. "To be conscious of others' suffering is to know compassion. It is in our love for others that we get to know ourselves. In a moment I will disappear. You will learn from suffering those lessons only your soul can teach you."

"Wait!" said Oberon, but Eugenia disappeared. Oberon was lost in the desert of a city where few plants grew. He knew he could sense north so he followed the heartbeat of the earth deep through the city. For mile after empty mile there was no food. Soon Oberon was too tired to fly and sat on a windowsill. His hunger was enormous. He did not know what his fate would be.

Oberon prayed to God. *Please give me strength. I know I should be learning, but I can't see what I am to learn from such a dire circumstance. My death will only prove that suffering surmounts all things.*

As Oberon was in mid-prayer, a small human girl trapped him in a jar. The girl shook the jar to make Oberon fly but he was too tired for that. He did not know whether his circumstances had improved or not. He gulped and expected his end.

Then Oberon noticed that the small human girl had no right leg. She hopped around on the only leg she had. *She must have known and still knows great suffering*, he thought.

Oberon took wing in the jar. The little girl's face lit up with joy. The girl hopped up the stairs and into the house with the butterfly jar. She showed the jar to her mother. Her mother looked and said, "That butterfly is hungry." She clipped a flower from her indoor plants and the little girl put the flower in the jar. Oberon's prayer was answered. He drank from the flower. Strength came back to him.

Oberon began to realize that it is important to depend on others for compassion. *I depended on the humans and the little girl depended on me. When we suffer we are completely dependant on others and their ability to understand our suffering. We must never be ashamed of our dependence. You depend on others so that others might depend on you someday.*

The little girl and her parents took their car and went out into the country. There the little girl released the butterfly from the jar. Oberon was free and he fluttered on the wind. Suffering, he realized, is only a moment; it fades at the margins but the memory lingers. We are not slaves to suffering—we were born for joy, after all—but suffering is inevitable.

At that moment Eugenia appeared. "In the midst of your suffering you found that your compassion for the little girl swept away all of your own hardship. What you gave took away your own suffering. It is in our love for others that the end to all suffering exists. Better than a prayer is to give compassion. It is only love that can lead into the sanctuary of heaven." Eugenia disappeared and Oberon did not see her again in this life.

In his last day Oberon sat on a leaf watching the sunrise. "I saw my own suffering and salvation. I saw love overcome all things. All that I experienced was in God's prism. But what am I? Am I something special? Or am I a monster?" With that last question the butterfly died.

Born again in midsummer, Oberon went through his phases from egg to caterpillar to chrysalis to butterfly. He remembered the last question he had asked before his death: Who was he, a lowly caterpillar or something special, a glorious butterfly?

Eugenia suddenly appeared next to him. "You do not know whether you are special or a monster, but it is all ego."

Oberon thought a moment. "It is ego to be a lowly caterpillar?"

"Yes, Oberon, it is all ego. You consider the caterpillar lowly because you think you are greater. You must not be great or lowly. You must be nothing. Nothing is the absence of something. Any something you are is an act of egoism. You must be absent of ego. Embrace the no-self, the nothing. In nothing is a vast emptiness. We cannot measure the emptiness but when we become nothing we become part of it. When you embrace nothingness, God will fill the emptiness and move wheresoever you move." Eugenia looked up at the cerulean blue sky. "Above is the sun, Oberon. Follow me and we will fly to it."

Higher and higher they went. But soon Oberon was exhausted. He looked at the sun and felt its warm rays on his face. Oberon stopped. "I cannot fly to the sun."

Eugenia nudged Oberon. "Try harder."

Oberon tried harder but still he could not reach the sun. Eugenia flew next to him. "What does it mean?" asked Oberon.

Eugenia replied, "It means no butterfly can reach the sun. Are you any less for not reaching your goal?"

Oberon looked at Eugenia. "I am disappointed I did not reach my goal, but I guess I am neither less nor more."

Eugenia smiled. "Though you thought your ego would be boosted, it was not affected in any way. When ego is unaffected you are in no-self, embracing the emptiness. You must not make attempts to gratify your ego or let failures diminish your ego. You must be absent of ego. This strengthens your soul and God will be with you. What are you, Oberon?"

Oberon smiled. "I am nothing, I am no-self, I am emptiness."

Eugenia disappeared, and Oberon continued north

with all the other monarch butterflies. He lived a full life for the next six weeks, until the day came for him to die again. The dawn fired its first arrow of light. Oberon sat on a leaf. He realized all at once that death was egoless. As he thought that, he died.

He had only one purpose when he was an egg and that was to become a caterpillar. As a caterpillar he had only one purpose, to become a chrysalis. He had only one purpose as a chrysalis and that was to become a butterfly. As he contemplated these thoughts, Eugenia appeared. "You are wondering what your purpose is."

Oberon looked at Eugenia. "All things have a purpose. What is mine? Life without purpose is futile."

Eugenia smiled. "You will know your purpose in time. God will lead you to your purpose as surely as the sun will dawn tomorrow. You will know your purpose not from the choice of ego but from the currents of circumstance. Things done to fulfill the ego eat away at your spirit. Your soul wanes like the dying moon."

The monarch butterflies went as far north as they would go. In the fall air the fourth generation began to die. Oberon sat on a leaf contemplating the dawn as he had done so many times before. Eugenia appeared beside him.

"Oberon, I have something to tell you. All these lives you have remembered and the lessons you've learned culminate with your next life. All we have done was meant to bring you to this point. In your next life you will live many times your current lifespan. You will be compelled to go south to the sacred ground almost a thousand miles away. But the sacred ground has been destroyed. Where your sacred ground once stood is now a human garbage dump. Without the sacred ground the monarch butterfly will become extinct in this part of the world. You can help us by leading the monarch butterfly to a new sacred ground. But we cannot compel you to do it."

Oberon looked at Eugenia. "God chose this purpose for me?" Oberon sighed. "There is a reason for my existence." He felt the darkness overwhelm him. The dawn opened like a flower. Like a stream his life flowed from his body. The cold touch of death claimed another butterfly.

Through every life Oberon had learned a lesson. First transience, then suffering, followed by no-self, then purpose. He wondered what lesson his fifth life would teach. When Oberon had reached the phase of a butterfly Eugenia appeared to him. She told him he had only one more lesson to learn.

"Can you make yourself worthy of the universe?" she asked him. "We are all judged by God. Not for the reasons we may think. God wants to better the universe. You have to ask yourself, how does my existence better the universe? Oberon, you have been given a special gift, to learn lessons in each life and remember and carry forward what you have learned. We have imbued you with the virtue of the universe."

Eugenia disappeared, and Oberon went about his task. He began by telling monarch butterflies that their sacred ground was gone and that they needed to follow him to a new one. They simply ignored him and continued on the path that beat in their hearts. Finally Oberon was compelled to tell them what Eugenia had told him. They all could sense Eugenia in their soul, for she was the mother of all the monarchs. But they knew she died long ago, and to claim to have seen her was insanity.

The more Oberon argued the less they listened. He could not make them see that they were headed for disaster. But Oberon would not give up. He kept trying to convince the monarch butterflies that their sacred ground did not exist. They traveled for a thousand miles and Oberon was still no closer to convincing them. Finally the migrating host of butterflies asked Oberon to leave. They told him he would not be allowed to share the sacred ground. He would be a wanderer without a home.

Reluctantly Oberon went his own way. His plan was to go to the garbage dump that was the former sacred ground before the entire host of butterflies got there. Once they realized he was right he could lead them to the new sacred ground. But as Oberon traveled, the wind began to pick up from the west and blew him off course. He knew that if he did not make it to the garbage dump before the host, chaos would ensue and the monarch butterflies could become extinct.

God, through the evolutionary engine, determines what species will live or die. Adaptation in this case was on the shoulders of one butterfly alone. Oberon knew he could not fail. He was determined to use all his strength to get to the garbage dump. Then the wind began to blow against him. He kept losing ground even as he went forward. The suffering he endured was tremendous. He thought his wings would be torn asunder. It began to rain and the water made his wings heavy. But Oberon fluttered forward.

At last, after many days of suffering, he reached his destination. The monarch butterflies were just starting to arrive. They were fluttering about chaotically, confused.

Oberon got their attention. He told them again that there was another sacred ground.

"Hear me! Change is the foremost part of the universe. You must not fear change. You must flow with change. Did you not change from egg to caterpillar, from caterpillar to chrysalis, from chrysalis to butterfly? This will be just another change."

Oberon waited for each butterfly to arrive at the garbage dump. With great compassion he filled their souls with strength. Then, when the entire host had arrived, Oberon led them to the new sacred ground. The monarch butterfly had been saved.

Months more passed and Oberon was reaching the end of his life. Eugenia appeared. She said, "This is your last life. You have done well. There is no more to be said."

Oberon sat on a leaf. The eye of dawn opened to a new day. Everything was quiet and still. The darkness began to swallow him. "I have learned so much and I have seen so many tomorrows. This is the last instant. My bravest moment, my last change. I will never be again. Everything fades. The last dawn. How warm the sun."

The great butterfly met his end as the sky opened and beams of light poured onto the spot where his lifeless body lay. But was it the end?

"I bring the good news of endless tomorrows," Eugenia said. "You have the universe's attention. You have broken your cycle of lives. God has asked you to join the host of angels. You will teach what you have learned. You have been judged worthy. Now you may join God in the core of the universe and exist without limits. Now you know life is only a veil. Once you have looked through, you discover that God was all there ever was."

THE WHITE SPIDER TRILOGY

The White Spider

The chronicles of Rodney Roach, volume one. Rex was born from the brood of the spider Natasha. He was unusual from the start. He was white as alabaster and his legs were like glass. There was an ancient prophecy among the spider clans that one day a white spider would come and lead them to the dominion of all the world. Many white spiders had come and gone, but the world would never forget Rex.

Natasha noticed he would not eat. The other young spiders would pounce on the prey Mother had provided, but Rex shunned all food. She took young Rex aside and showed him the food. "Here it is—you need not compete. Here, I have taken off the head for you. All you have to do is suck." Rex stepped back in revulsion. "But you are a spider—you must eat live food," said Natasha. Rex screamed, "I will not kill and I will not partake in killing." "But you are a spider—you must kill to survive. It is your place to reduce the numbers of other creatures that eat other things." "I will not hunt and I will not feast on the blood of those I have murdered!" Rex ran out her sight. He kept running. He was running away from his mother, from his home, from the very idea of what a spider was. He kept running, and soon his home was far away, his

41

mother was far away, but he still was a spider. He said to himself, "I will never go back. My home is not a lair of killers. I must find a good place where goodness is possible and food is not the loss of life but the nourishment of living, not at a cost of a life but for the purpose of giving life." He wandered the wasteland of the house and found nothing to eat. He tasted dust, but it did not nourish him. Each day he wandered. He was growing weak from deprivation. At last he began to make webs and eat the filaments. Though this gave him a full belly, it would not nourish him. At long last he found some roaches. He stalked them just like prey. He was hungry, so hungry. Maybe the spider in him would defeat his better resolve.

The roaches went under the refrigerator. They were calmly feasting on crumbs of food. What was food? Was it a fat, succulent roach or a crumb of bread covered in mold? Rex pounced. He landed on the crumbs and began to devour them. The roaches froze of sheer fright. I was one of them, I remember.

But we were taken aback that he was eating the crumbs and not us. I began to laugh.

"What's this, a vegetarian spider?" Rex looked at me with one of eight eyes. "It's good I'm hungry." "What's wrong? I'm not good enough? Too skinny?" Rex laughed. "No, you're fat enough. I refuse to kill, yet I do need to eat." I looked at him. "This is a trick, right? You're toying with me and saving me for later." "No. I will not harm you. What is your name?"

I laughed. "The diner asks the meal what his name is . . . Well, it's Rodney." "Well, Rodney, I am Rex, and I need you to show me how to find food so I can survive." I, Rodney, snickered. "We don't keep our predators alive; it's just one of those things with us." Rex looked at Rodney with all eight eyes. "If you help me I will help you." Rodney raised one antenna. "I give you food, and what will you give me in return?" "I will protect you and your friends from other predators." Rodney thought a moment. "I thought you won't kill." "I don't have to kill to protect you." Rodney crossed his feet. "Make a roach square." Rex crossed his feet. Rodney looked at Rex. "Promises we keep, each day we eat until we reach that sleep."

Cooperation is special in its nature. Creatures that cooperate have a unique kinship with each other. But they are all of the same species. This was different; we were free to choose to be friends, enemies, or food and predator. But we chose to be each other's strength, and that made us both stronger. We grew up together. We shared our lives freely and drew a bounty that few gather in all their lives. We dubbed Rex "Super Roach." He protected us from all predators—they were simply stone scared of him. He had no nose for our food; he was meant to hunt and kill, not scavenge the ground for crumbs. We did all the searching, and he watched out for all predators with senses so keen and profound that we were always in awe of his powers.

One day, as we were minding our own business, we heard a cry for help. We moved slowly, as we knew not the danger that confronted us. Between the credenza and the wall was a female centipede. She was formed by some special grace, and if you could say that centipedes were beautiful, she was the pearl of their oyster. She was surrounded by three spiders. They were Rex's brothers. I looked at Rex. "Nothing here for us." "Those are my brothers." "Nothing here for us unless you want to join them in their feast." Rex looked at the centipede. "I cannot let her die." I shook my head. "It's none of our business, and we have food to find and the rest of our lives to slumber and sleek." Rex looked at me with all eight eyes. "The loss of one light, though it be on the horizon, diminishes us all." With that, he moved with all his spider speed under the credenza. The three spiders moved in on the centipede. They decided amongst themselves which one would lay the fatal strike. The chosen brother was about to pounce when he heard a voice. "You go no further," said Rex boldly. His brother snickered and pounced anyway. He landed on the centipede. Suddenly spider silk tied his mandibles shut. The other two brothers turned to fight. "Tell Mother I am fine," said Rex. Then he moved with such speed and grace that the brothers were left all but standing still. He wrapped silk round each of their mandibles. They fled in disarray. He walked with all eight translucent feet toward the centipede. The sunshine shone behind him, and if you looked from the centipede's view you would have seen a white spider walking on rays of light. The centipede said, "Are you an angel?" She looked again. "But you are a spider." Rex said softly, "I will not hurt you. What is your name?" "My name is Estella. Who are you?" Rodney stood in front of Rex. "He is Rex. He defends the weak and protects the wise." Rodney laughed and said, "We call him Super Roach." Estella looked in amazement at Rex. "These are your friends." Rex smiled. "They are my family." "But they are roaches and . . . and you are a spider." She moved with infinite grace and delicate beauty as she looked up close at Rex. "You don't look like any spider I have ever seen. What are you?" She looked away and at Rodney and the other roaches. "No. I was right when I first saw you.

You are an angel." Rex smiled. "Are you far from home?" She leaned close and kissed Rex on the cheek. "I am very far from home. My home is a place of many moods, unlike the one solemn mood of yours. It is outside in the garden. There are three rocks. Two that hold the sky and one that shelters my soul. The mood we are in now is the sad mood. All is white. It is cold and barren. That is why I enter the house during this mood. But all the other moods are the seasons that feed my spirit. For one bad mood I would not give up my garden and my sheltering soul." She looked at Rex and his tribe. "Do you have a home?" I, Rodney, looked at her. "We wander from place to place. It's never safe enough to stay in one place very long. Even with Super Roach we have enemies that we cannot defend against," Rex said. "Maybe one day you will show us your home." Estella looked into Rex's eyes. "Maybe you will come and stay and never want to return to this dry, solemn land of yours." I could see it. It was easy to see. that the attraction between Estella and Rex transcended all boundaries. They were not of the same species. There was nothing similar about them except a certain something in their souls. Maybe God made bodies different than he made souls. Some souls are similar, though the mask is all differences. And though the body is all the same, the soul has different gravities. What makes us what we are is the stuff of miracles and the element of dreams. But love has no boundaries and no limits in its circumference to make us more than we are and perhaps more of what we really are in our souls.

Winter is a cold hand. It touches all things with death's own fingers. On the coldest day of the year, the moisture of the nearby lake caused frost and icicles to grow like the stalagtites of some heavenly cavern. In this landscape we were vulnerable. Our hard shells could not protect us from the cold winter wind. To keep us warm and safe, Rex wrapped us in his silk. This served us immobile, but at least we would not freeze to death.

Estella looked at Rex. "What about you?" Rex smiled. "I will bear it. My blood is fast; it will outrun the winter cold. And while you are wrapped like this I must protect you with all my strength." As he was finishing wrapping Estella he heard a noise behind him. There, standing before him, was a huge female spider. The female was a cousin of Rex's named Matilda. "Rex, you have prepared a feast for us." Rex looked at Estella. "I'll be right back." Rex stood in front of the huge female. She was almost three times his size. "Are you coming to mate, Rex?" Matilda said. "No, Matilda. I'm coming to fight." She laughed. "I heard about you, the vegetarian spider. You make me ashamed. Those creatures are beneath you. Spiders are superior— that is why we feast on them and not them on us." Rex stepped forward. "We are equal. Equality makes us dependent aponupon each other. They are my friends. Our strength means we have a greater responsibility to those that are weaker than us. It is our obligation." "What obligation? Your first obligation is to your fellow spiders. You are a traitor to our species." With that, Rex closed her mandibles with silk. But she broke free and pounced on Rex. Her enormous body weight held him down. "If we had mated I would have eaten you, but now I will enjoy your flesh anyway."

Rex was helpless under her strength. Her fangs drew nearer and nearer. Her copious venom dripped on Rex's skin. She was about to bite when Estella screamed, "*Rex!*"

Matilda growled, distracted, and at that moment Rex kicked with all his might. Rex and Matilda tumbled backwards and slid down the ice and out of sight. Several moments passed, and then we saw a great shadow approaching us. It was Matilda. Estella began to cry. I felt our doom sealed as we were sealed in these pouches. Suddenly Matilda fell down in a great crash and you could see a sharp icicle impaled in her back. The morning light shone into the house. Like the very sun, Rex walked forward with the dawn in every leg. "My angel," said Estella. "If I lost you . . ." Estella wrapped her body round Rex and Rex stroked her lightly with his legs. I looked at Rex. "You killed." Rex looked at me and at the other roaches. "Killing is wrong," Rex said, "but sometimes you have no other choice. If your life and the life of your friends depend on it, then it is all you can do. Extinguishing the light of life must be avoided if it can be. If you cannot defend yourself you will die, and that serves nobody. If you kill to defend others, that serves the light of survival. When it is between your light and the light of another one, you can only choose your own light. You must be your champion and the champion of others. Nothing grants us peace but our strength. Nothing grants us life but our will to survive."

The light found its way back home. Spring rose from its wintry ashes. We who had no home followed Estella to hers. "What is a home?" I thought. "Where do wandering souls find rest?" I saw the sky, and it was big. I saw the sun, and its warmth held me close like a long lost child. The flowers were a cathedral and their scent the incense burning on the altar of a better day. The day we went home. It was like Estella described two stones that held the sky and one stone on top to shelter the soul. Rex smiled. "This is a fortress." He climbed on top and could see the lake and the surrounding trees. He made a tangled web and kept making it and making it. I asked what he was doing and he just smiled. At last he showed us what he was working on. He put it at the entrance to our home. Estella looked at it and said, "What a beautiful star." It was a web in the shape of a star, and when the light shone on it it glowed with the reflections and was a shining star to compete with the heavens. Rex looked at Estella. "This place is the place of Estella, and this is her star to signify how we shall honor her home and honor each other. Stars do not occur without effort. It is the measure of effort that defines how bright the star."

Rex began a reconnaissance of the surrounding area. I went with him and we looked for what could become our source of nourishment. We watched the butterflies consume the nectar, but we had not the wings for that. Then we saw ants. They were carrying wheat. Rex went stalking them like prey. He pounced on one of the ants. I heard him scream, "My comrades will avenge me!" Rex smiled. "No need. I will not eat you." "You are a spider." "I am different. I eat what you eat. I want to know where you are getting the food from." The ant looked at Rex. "You are a strange one. The adjoining farm grows wheat and we harvest it for the mound. It is ours we will not share!" "I will make a compact with you if you will lead me to your queen." "We make no deals with spiders." But he led us to his queen nevertheless. I was really worried. If the ants wanted to destroy us, they could effortlessly overwhelm us with numbers. Rex looked straight into the enormous queen's eyes and said, "I will give you my protection in return for sharing the wheat." The queen scoffed. "We need no spider's protection. We have majors." The majors with their enormous mandibles moved forward. In an instant Rex moved and closed their mandibles shut with spider silk. The queen put her antennae back. "Yes, but it is the sheer numbers that win the day for us every time." Rex looked at the queen. "But alone and carrying your wheat you are defenseless; by the time the numbers arrive, your comrades have already been devoured." Rex threw a wheat grain toward the mound ceiling. Before the queen could catch it, he had moved three times round her and caught the grain before she could even blink. "My, my, my," she said. "You are an extraordinary creature. We ants can protect ourselves, but I think this spider could more aggressively protect our crop. My word is my compact." Rex nodded. "My word is also my compact. You will not regret having me in your service. If I serve you, you will serve me. We must depend upon each other; in this way we can prosper more greatly."

As we, the roaches, were carrying the wheat back to Estella, this enormous wasp appeared. He was blue—so blue he was black. The ants and all of us roaches dropped our wheat and went to find a place to hide. But not all could escape. The wasp shot down like a rocket and was about to snatch a helpless ant when Rex interposed himself between the wasp and the ant. The wasp landed. "Saving dinner for yourself, Mr. Spider. Look, I am wise. My name is Achilleas. We can share—there are plenty of ants for both of us. It will save us a big fight." "I am Rex, and, Mr. Achilleas, I will not allow you to harm these ants."

Achilleas put his antennae back. "You are protecting them! Then what do you eat?" "I eat the same as them." Achilleas shook his head. "That sustains you." Rex smiled. "It is all I need." Achilleas looked into Rex's eyes. "You protect the weak?" "I defend the weak, and they feed me. There is a balance to our relationship." Achilleas fluttered his wings. "Teach me. I want to be like you." Rex looked with all eight eyes at the sleek, armored Achilleas. "The strong have a responsibility to the weak. It is our trust. The strong were put here by God for the sake of the weak. If we abuse our strength, we hurt ourselves, for the weak will not benefit us further. Killing is wrong except in self-defense. We powerful creatures must live by stronger rule by principle, which makes us just and ennobles our actions." Achilleas learned. The whole garden learned. Achilleas became the first knight in the service of our King Rex, for Estella became a kingdom and the shining star brought new light to creatures' eyes. The moths and the butterflies shared nectar with us, and nectar became the wine of our nation. Grasshoppers, ladybugs, aphids, so many joined our community of mutual assistance. Hearing of the new order, wasps and spiders came to live vegetarian lives as knights in the service of King Rex.

This was a place that every creature dreamed of in his sleeping hours. The land of possibility. Hope made manifest. We who lived to suffer and die. To struggle without purpose for every ounce of our survival. We had found a meaning to our existence. In that star was not just hope, but the reason why life was invented. King Rex had built the kingdom of paradise. We need not wait for our share of heaven after death, for here in the light of this king's ambition was a new Jerusalem that did not fade.

Heaven's gates were open to all who could grasp the consequence of the meaning of that one star. It was our salvation.

Then the bees came. Nobody knows whence they came. I remember the day when they made their surprise attack. The morning dew that day clung to the star and fell in drops to the earth. It was as if the star were crying. So many died. The suffering was overwhelming. Like some dark cloud from the abyss, they descended upon our kingdom Estella. The knights were helpless—there were too many. The king convened a council at the rock. "This is war!" screamed the multitude. "The bees must pay for this atrocity," said an elder grasshopper.

Rex looked at all his people. "We all lost a friend, a brother, a sister, a mother. We have been attacked without provocation. Yet we must hope for a better way to end this misunderstanding. I cannot fathom that this is purely an act of irreconcilable evil. Yet we shall prepare for war." The multitude cheered. Suddenly one single bee flew into the rock and arrogantly stood before the king. "Kill him!" screamed the multitude. "Kill him!"

The king said, "Let him speak." "The queen has sent me. This is a formal declaration of war. We were forced by your selfish and defiant ambitions to attack and destroy you. We shall proceed until you have left these lands or have been utterly vanquished." Rex asked angrily, "What selfish and defiant ambitions? We have no ambitions on your hive!" The bee boldly looked at Rex. "Your moths and butterflies are consuming all the nectars in this country, and we are being left barren. Our survival depends upon your annihilation."

Rex shook his head in sorrow. "This is a terrible

mistake. We are willing to share the nectar with you. We did not know that you were being endangered by our gathering of these nectars. We can negotiate an end to this conflict. Let me talk to your queen." The bee laughed. "We will not share with you, and you will not talk to our queen. You cannot look upon her! She is holy. She is sacred. You would desecrate our culture. Your very notions are madness." "Then you shall be my intermediary." The bee laughed again. "I do not talk to the queen. She talks to me. You may kill me at your leisure. I am only here to convey a message. Nothing more." "Kill him!" screamed all the Estellans. Rex shook his head. "No. You may have come with suicidal intent. But my intentions are good. I seek no revenge. You may go." Then the bee stung himself and fell dead before the king. Queen Estella looked at Rex. "What kind of creatures are these?" "I don't know, my love, but there must be a better way. Reason must be the standard by which we measure our interactions. Without reason we are left to brute force. If we could only communicate with each other, the killing would stop." Small skirmishes persisted between the bees and the estellans. Days passed and the king sat thinking as the nation prepared for a desperate struggle. He then convened another council. "The bees have overwhelming numbers and aerial superiority. We have only one chance in order to win. A small raiding party must covertly enter the hive. The queen is the center of the bees' lives; without her they are without compass. We will either negotiate a peace or vanquish her. It is our only chance for survival." The king looked round at his knights. "This may be suicide, so I am only asking for volunteers. I, myself, am the first volunteer." Achilleas stepped forward. "I am with you, King." I, Rodney, stepped forward. "I will carry the food." A small party of spiders, wasps, and ant majors was brought together. They were the hive raiders. They were our last hope.

On the day we left for the journey, Estella came ready to go with us. "I am coming with you." Rex looked at her. "You are staying. This is too dangerous. If we do not return, you, the queen of Estella, must guide these people out of the garden to a new place and a new hope." "If you do not return, then my heart will melt in sorrow and my existence will be dust for the devouring wind." Rex kissed Queen Estella. "Then I must come home."

"I will never forgive you if you do not." "Will we ever see each other again?" Rex said, tapping his feet softly on her. She wrapped herself round. "In the will of your heart is the road back to me." They kissed one last time. Then the journey began. Journeys are like the wandering course of a soul in search of God. It begins with fear. The darkness, the unknown, is all around; there is only the hope of God, that light we carry in our souls that guides us forward, guides us into the gates of heaven toward the longing quest that drives our soul. The bees were everywhere patrolling the entrance to the hive tree. Its shadow was long. Its dark arms reached the sky and the eye of the hive was an all-seeing eye of doom. We went round the lake's edge, following its boundary. The tree had roots that lay in the lake. We were certain that if we came from the opposite direction from the very lake itself that it would be unguarded. But how to cross the lake undetected?

We saw Rex dive into the lake. Bubbles rose from the

waters. "What is he doing?" said Achilleas. "I don't know," I said. Then one great bubble rose to the surface. Inside the bubble was the king. Spiders are God's greatest achievement, of this I am sure. Each spider carried a wasp, ant major, or roach. They would gather in the bubbles, and with the dexterity they use in making webs, they would build the bubble round us. The currents of the lake carried us toward the tree. Fish swam by. They were ugly beasts without remorse. One bubble was consumed entirely into the depths of the lake by one of these aquatic beasts. We lost friends. But the journey continued. As we floated we could see the moon on the waters. The light of the moon lit the translucent legs of Rex, and it was as if our party of bubbles followed some star that was hidden beneath the waves. Hidden beneath a veil that would deliver us from certain doom.

On reaching the tree, we rose to the surface near the knotty shore of roots that lingered in the lake's lip. Sleeping there was a party of bees. We moved slowly, and in an instant we were on them, slaughtering them. "Let not one escape and give alarm, or we are lost!" Some bees headed up the tree; Achilleas and the other wasps made chase. They flew daringly and at great speed through the heart of the tree. Another band of bees was making their escape up another entrance. The king screamed, "Spider silk on the escape!" All the spiders fired silk together and the exit was sealed. The bees became entangled and were promptly killed. Achilleas chased a bee in and out through the knotty entrails of the tree. He was the last bee. There was a hole ahead, and if the bee reached it the mission would be lost. Achilleas found the extra power in the spark of his spirit. He darted forward. He had one chance, and that was as the bee slowed to enter the hole; he could not miss. He came in fast, he lanced the bee on his stinger, and it was over. Achilleas and the wasps returned to where Rex and the rest of the raiders waited. They quickly moved deep into the tree. The paths were confusing. They led many directions. Rex led us with his spider senses, but soon it became too confusing for even his great ability.

Lucky for us, at that moment we found a cricket in the middle of the path. "Who goes there?" said the cricket. He was about to make a sound when Rex pounced on him. "Don't kill me," said the cricket. "I must chirp every hour to tell the bees that nobody comes this way. If I do not, they will kill you," I said to Rex. "He must be telling the truth, for I heard a chirp exactly an hour ago." Rex let him chirp. Then Rex looked at the cricket with all eight eyes. "Which way to the hive?" The cricket gulped. "That path there on the right will take you straight to the back of the hive." Then the raiders made their way up the path. The cricket waited for them to go, then started to snicker under his breath and headed toward the left path. Suddenly a wasp lance impaled the cricket. I said to Rex, "How did you know it was a trick?" "I smelled the royal jelly on his breath. Only the most trusted and loyal would have access to the same food that feeds the queen." We made our way within the hour to the back of the hive. Here was the entrance that would lead us directly to the queen. The moonlight shone through each shaft. It was a miracle of engineering, geometric and precise. Each hexagon lit bright by moonlight was a path to our destiny. We broke into small teams. Rex, Achilleas, and I made one team. We knew not what team would succeed. We wished each other safe passage into the next world. This was our moment. It was the call of fate.

Into the breach we went. If we were discovered at any point we would be dead. We moved quietly. The smell of honey was so profound that it sickened my sensibilities.

We moved through passage after passage. We dispatched the bees in our path. But we had to be careful. Zzzzzz, and a bee popped out of the corner. I jumped. It barely missed me with its stinger. Rex closed its mouth with silk before it could make an alarm, and Achilleas killed it with one sting. Every moment was tense. Every passage ended not at the queen's retreat, but elsewhere. We kept looking. Then what we had all feared occurred.

Zzzzzzz, then screams from our comrades. Zzzzzzz, and a battle ensued. We began moving fast as the alarm was being given; soon it would reach the queen. Zzzzzzzzzzz.

Bees began to chase us down the passage. Zzzzzzzzzz. I heard my lifelong friend Zippy scream. That day I lost all my childhood roach friends. Zzzzzzzzzzzzz. We saw an exit up ahead. Zzzzzzzzzzzzzzzz. The bees were right behind us. We made it though the exit, and there before us, big as life, was the queen. Zzzzzzzzzzzzzzzzzzzzzzzzzzzzzzzzzzzzzzzzzzzzzzz.

We were surrounded— it was over. All our comrades were already dead. We would be dead soon. Zzzzzzzzz. "Wait!" screamed Rex. "I am here to negotiate a treaty if you are willing." "You desecrate my being with eight eyes and you want to negotiate. You are mad!" "My purpose is to make peace. Let me speak; then you may do as you will with us, for we have desecrated willfully your most holy shrine." Zzzzzzzzzzzzzzz. "Speak, spider." Rex looked away from the queen with his eyes down. "We are at war not because we deserve such a fate, but because we cannot fully communicate across our cultural boundaries. You are a race built on reason. The very geometry of your hive and the organization of your tribe is defined by reason. I ask you to be reasonable to see beyond our differences and see the possibilities. We can share the cultivation of nectar to each kingdom's benefit. We were ignorant that we were causing you any suffering. We would not knowledgably cause the suffering of any beings. It is not our way." Zzzzzzzz.

"Spider, you speak wisely. War must be avoided if we have the will. We will make this treaty with you in exchange for your lives. For you have looked upon me, and that is a crime that must be punished." Rex looked at his friends. "We are a worthy sacrifice for a better world, and we willingly surrender to your justice." Zzzzzzzz. Just then the alarm was sounded. Just then an army began to pour onto the tree. It was myriads upon myriads. No creature could imagine the sheer number and mass of this host. At the head was a centipede on a Luna moth. The sky was filled with wasps of every kind. The bees looked at the queen. "We cannot survive this. We are finished." "We must surrender," said the queen. The queen bee surrendered to King Rex. The war was over. The dawn rose over the garden in all its golden glory.

Queen Estella stepped off her Luna moth and jumped into Rex's arms. "Where did all these people come from?" Estella kissed Rex. "They all heard you were in trouble. They all came to help from the neighboring gardens and farms as far as the eye can see and the mind can dream. They all heard of King Rex and his kingdom Estella. 'This cannot pass away from this earth,' they all said. 'It is our only hope. It is our salvation. If we lost this kingdom we would lose the only gift that God has ever bestowed upon us.'" She wrapped around Rex. "I could not let that last kiss be my last memory of you. I need your soul to shelter me. You are my only home and harbor." "I thought for a moment that I would never see you again. Now we are home." The multitude gathered to hear the king speak. Many had come so far and dreamt so long for their deliverance that they thirsted for the great spider to lay his healing words on their ears. Rex looked out at the great host. "Today begins a fresh flowering of my kingdom Estella. I named it after my queen, for it is what I love most. My eternal service is yours. As long as I have breath I will be your comfort, be your guide, be your king. I lit a candle in the darkness. Others gathered my light and lit their own candles. This is the candle of hope. If you light a thousand candles, you will build a star. It will shine with the power of people's hopes. It will shine with the power of people's dreams. Each day this star shines brighter. Remember how brightly it shines, and above all, remember that to build an everlasting star you start with just one candle."

The kingdom flourished in a golden light. It was the pinnacle of people's dreams.

Many stories have been told of this place, but they can never equal the luster of having lived in its soft grace. One day a darkness came over the great spider. Rex fell to bed. He could barely move, and the light in his eight eyes was beginning to dim. I was there in his last moments. There were no heirs, as the queen and king could not have children. He was asked who would be the next king. He said only, "I leave the kingdom to the wisest."

Achilleas came to the king. "What will I do in a world without a King Rex? Who will guide me to the right?" "Achilleas, the right is your very compass. I did not make you a knight; you were always a knight." I was one of the last other than the queen to see the king breathing. I looked at the dying king and said, "Super . . . Roach . . ." He looked at me and made a roach square. "Promises we keep, each day we eat, until we reach that sleep."

I made a roach square. Rex smiled. "That sleep has come, and I need your promise more than ever. This kingdom will fade if the flames are not fanned. Don't let the starlight fade into memory. All we have done is not finished. If I had more life to live I would make this the universal star that joins the distant to the close . . . Don't let this idea die with me."

I looked at Rex. "Super Roach, I need your promise. Don't linger in the darkness; come back to us soon." Rex closed his eyes. "How can I promise what I do not know?" I looked at Rex. "If it is up to you, return . . . return . . ." I began to sob. The king called his queen Estella. "My love, I am leaving home . . . I don't know when I will return." He touched her softly with his legs. "I am coming soon, my love . . . Without my angel there is no more sheltering soul." She wound round him in a tight embrace. The light shone into the rock, the star lit up with a spectrum of colors, and the king floated on his own bed of light. One realized that moment that star and king were the same thing.

Estella said, "Until tomorrow's kiss." She bent over and kissed Rex, and his last breath filled her soul. The king was gone. A great star had vanished from the heavens. But the idea lives, and as embers of a fire they await his return

to light up our world with its grace.
    If we are lucky. Someday . . . Someday.

Achilleas

The chronicles of Rodney Roach, volume two. He was dark as the midnight sky, armored like the toughest beetle, and fast as yesterday's dreams. Achilleas was a blue mud dauber wasp, and he was the greatest knight of the kingdom of Estella. There are many stories we could tell just of Estella, for it was where King Rex, the white spider, ruled. It was the once and shining hope for all nature. There was a place where all insects lived together serving each other's needs. Where the strong protected the weak and where all insects cooperated for their mutual benefit. It was heaven on earth. We were all lucky to have lived there if only for a brief moment. Achilleas's deeds were part of public folklore. He was a legend. But he could not find enough for him in being a legend. He wanted more. Achilleas was in search of himself. I would sit with him as we looked to the lake and far across. "Those are distant lands," he would say. "Nothing but forest, nothing there for us," I would say. "Far away is my soul, and I must find it one day." "Is not the kingdom enough for you?" He looked at me. "I have found purpose, but not a meaning that defines this purpose. I serve Rex because it is the right thing to do. I derived satisfaction from being the first knight. But now I am empty. I need something." I smiled. "You need a female wasp." Achilleas began to laugh. "You may just be right." He continued being the great Achilleas, but the feeling would not go away, and soon he was before Rex and his queen Estella. "I ask permission to leave the kingdom." Rex smiled. "You need no permission to leave this kingdom. Freedom is about choices and the liberty to make those choices. If I were to command you to stay, I would steal your liberty. You come and go as you choose, not I." Achilleas smiled. "Then we shall part company, for I shall go." Rex looked at Achilleas with all eight eyes. "Where will you be going?" "To the farthest side of the lake and beyond." Queen Estella said, "That is unexplored and very far." Rex walked up to Achilleas. "But our friend, if you must go find peace in your soul, and if you ever return, your place in our society is open." The queen said, "And your friends will be so thirsty to see you. Come back soon." Rex smiled. "I will tell you what I tell all the knights. Achilleas, good friend . . . seek kindness." Achilleas looked at the star and it shone bright in the sunshine. It was the famous web of Rex. The king's star. It meant so many things to so many people. Achilleas said, "May I never forget this star." Then he zoomed into the sky, and I thought I might never see him again. We all thought so. The following story I tell as Achilleas told me. He flew across the lake. The wind was behind him, and he felt his whole life before him. Maybe, he thought, this was his destiny. To wander the far side of the lake and explore. He had always wandered alone. This would be no different. As he flew he felt the moisture from the lake, and he heard a voice in his soul. "There can only be one star." He ignored the voice and went on until he reached the mysterious shoreline of the far side of the lake. It smelled different, of pine and elm and oak. He was mindful of all he had learned from Rex. Protecting the weak, the role of the strong in the universe was to serve those that were weaker. Death was the final option, not the first. The kingdom was part of him, and he felt it would serve him well as he traveled. As a knight of Estella, he could not hunt for food. Theirs was a vegetarian way. A gentle way. Death was not part of nourishment. Killing for food had been abolished. He was hungry, so he found some berries to eat. This would not be hard at all, he thought. Food is plentiful, and there is so much undiscovered country. His soul, he felt, was unfolding from its sleep. He felt at peace.

Suddenly he heard a distress call from a wasp. He moved with great speed. He found a large spider had trapped a wasp. Achilleas engaged the spider. The spider hit Achilleas with silk. This got caught in his wings. Achilleas came crashing to the ground. The spider moved forward for the kill. In a flash, Achilleas took again to the air and surprised the spider with his speed. The spider screamed. But Achilleas lanced him and killed him, then and there. The other wasp thanked Achilleas. "Now we can share the spider as a meal." Achilleas shook his head. "I do not partake of killing for food. I am Estellan. We only eat fruit and grain, no meat." "Oh, that is a pity. Such a juicy spider," said the wasp. The wasp looked up at the sky. "Vanusha will be angry if we do not eat this spider. By eating the spider we eat the sun. The sun nourishes our soul. The spider is not dead. He will return to the sun and be reborn. But by partaking of the spider, we learn from the spider. It is only in death that life can be made." Achilleas looked at the wasp. "Where did you learn this from?" The wasp looked at the sky. "From Vanusha, my goddess. She is the sun. She is the moon. She is eternity." "We Estellans believe that life nourishes life. Death is a path that must be avoided." The wasp laughed. "You cannot avoid death. Death is part of life. Life is a vessel carried by death's wind. We are not meant to live without death as our spiriting force. It is only through death that we grow stronger. It is only in strength that we can have the spirit of the wasp within, and through this spirit we are elevated. For wasps were meant to rule the land, not just survive. It is our destiny." Achilleas watched the wasp devour the spider. The words were seductive. He had never heard these ideas before. Could death be the true source of life? Could Rex have been wrong? Perhaps killing was the way to extol life. Perhaps wasps have a higher destiny than other insects. He had never heard of a wasp goddess. This was what he had been looking for: To elevate his spirit in new ways. To find what it meant to be a wasp.

The wasp finished devouring the spider and said, "I will take you to Vanusha. She will want to meet you. That spider had devoured six wasps before you killed it." Achilleas shook his head. "I thought you said Vanusha was a goddess." "She is. You will see." The wasp introduced himself as Hector. He was a monk in the service of Vanusha. He spread the teachings of Vanusha to other wasps and taught wasp lore to the young.

Achilleas followed the wasp through the forest. There were streams and waterfalls and wild flowers. They followed an incline and the hill led to a great oak tree. It seemed to reach deep into the heavens. And as Achilleas approached the oak tree, the leaves began to rustle. The very rustle was a voice. It was the voice of God. Wasps of all kinds made this place their home. This was a wasp paradise. The place that wasps dreamt of when they were born. The quest of every wasp soul.

Achilleas landed on a branch. There before him was a beautiful wasp with the most slender, curvaceous body he had ever seen. "Who is that?" said Achilleas. "That is

Roxanne, a priestess of Vanusha." She did a dance— it was slow and seductive. It was a dance of life and a dance of death. It was a dance of love. It was a dance of eternity.

Suddenly he saw a star high in the oak tree. Achilleas wondered what that was. As the star descended, he noticed it was a strange wasp. It was transparent and had a whip for a tail. She landed before an unconscious spider. She looked straight at Achilleas as if recognizing him. The spider revived. She walked over to it. In that moment there began a staring contest between the spider and the wasp. The spider was transfixed by the wasp's eyes. Suddenly the whip tail struck and the spider fell dead. She sat on the spider and deposited eggs. Achilleas looked at Hector. Hector responded, "That is Vanusha." Then Vanusha moved forward to the crowd. She stopped in front of Achilleas. "Welcome to our paradise, stranger. What brings you here?" Achilleas looked at Vanusha. "I come in search of myself." "You will find what you seek here. All wasps will find the journey ends at Vanusha." "Is death the purpose of life?" asked Achilleas. She looked up close at him. "What are your wings for?" "To fly, of course." "No. To kill. Your wings, your senses are built to destroy, not preserve. Only your armor preserves your soul. All else is the blade that deals death. You were meant to kill. Only in death can you build your life." Achilleas thought a moment. "All my life was meant for death only." Vanusha looked up toward the sky. "Not death only. The sky was built on death. Nothing so large could exist without the element of death. Death is not just the food of life, it is the food of everything. The sun is the ultimate killer, and it lies above even the sky. Each death is an incarnation of the sun. Just like the light of the sun slays the darkness at dawn, each one of us slays something as well. Like the sun, we shine from the death we have caused." Achilleas looked up at the sun shining bright in the sky. "Do we live again?" Vanusha smiled and her eyes were suddenly deeply hypnotizing. "We live again like the sun vanquished by the moon lives again and slays the moon, and just as darkness slays the light and light slays darkness. These are no coincidences. It is death speaking to us." Vanusha looked deep into Achilleas's eyes. "Follow us in paradise. You will not be sorry." Vanusha brushed her body seductively against Achilleas. The great blue wasp was confused, but he continued his stay in the land of Vanusha. He learned their ways. He began to eat flesh. He began to hunt and kill. Sunrises and sunsets were never so red. He thought to himself that this was the color of death, and death was the conqueror over life. This twilight hour he would spend seated in the high oak overwhelmed by the power of death. How could Rex be so wrong? He thought, "Rex is so confused he believes that life begets life, and only the values of life can bring life to others." Achilleas remembered Rex's words. "If we destroy life we diminish the world. All life has value, and this treasure must be preserved if one can. We were not given by God in the name of death, but to protect ourselves and others from death. Only in grave danger must we take life, for each memory in that life is irreplaceable. Should we take life, we must find forgiveness from the God inside. If you kill for pleasure, it is evil without measure." Those last words hurt the most and were repeated over and over in the soul of Achilleas. He had killed not just once but over and over again. He believed in his heart that he had become evil without measure, just as Rex had said. In the summer came the June bugs. This brought on a frenzy of killing. Vanusha would scream each morning, "Don't come back until each June bug has met his July." The killing was beyond comprehension. Thousands of June bugs would be feasted on each day. Achilleas flew about eating June bugs like the other Vanushans. But on one day as he flew in for a kill he heard a June bug screaming on his back legs in the air. "Memory of God," he screamed. "All that I am is gone like the flowers of spring. Everything I know will vanish with me. What am I, God, just a collection of memories that will never be again. Save me so that I might remember my salvation." Achilleas stood over the June bug, his stinger ready for the kill. The June bug began to cry. "This is my fate, to fall like the autumn leaf. This is my last memory of life." Instead of striking, Achilleas lifted the beetle into the sky and took him away. He landed far away with the beetle in his grasp. The June bug opened one eye and looked around. He heard Achilleas's voice. "You're safe, nobody will hurt you." "You spared my life?" Achilleas looked nervously around. "I did not spare you. You spared me. Until I heard you I had forgotten the reason for life being so precious is the treasure of memory. Our experience of life is unique. It should not be hurriedly destroyed. Maybe life is more profound and valuable than death." The June bug looked at Achilleas. "Noble wasp, you are wrong. Only our own memories and perceptions are valuable; those of others is fodder for the enduring power of death. My philosophy is that my personal life is valuable none others. If I had your power to destroy other memories, I would vanquish them day and night. In life one must be selfish, not selfless. I never thought for one second that my life should be given up for others, but only for myself. We are here today and gone tomorrow. My life is only valuable to me, to no other. If I could destroy you as you meant to do with me, I would never hesitate." Achilleas only turned and left the beetle where he was never to see him again. The entire exchange confused the wasp further. He had thought for a moment Rex was right. But Rex would only spit at him now. He could not agree with Vanusha completely, but there was no return to Estella. He was an outcast.

For many months Vanusha would spend time talking to Achilleas of Estella. She would pump him for information but avoid the differing philosophy. Vanusha would consume his time day by day. But Achilleas was not consumed by Vanusha; he was rather more interested in Roxanne. Each night he would follow Roxanne to the very top of the great oak tree. There he would silently watch her as she bathed in the glow of the starry sky. For many months he just watched. During daylight, Roxanne would ignore his advances. This was very frustrating to Achilleas. So he resolved to speak to her during her trip to the top of the great oak. There she was standing in the moonlight looking across the sky at the stars. Achilleas walked up behind her. "The stars remind me of my home country, Estella." Roxanne turned around and smiled. "The stars remind me that dreams do continue to shine, though we are living here. Do you miss your homeland?" Achilleas joined Roxanne at the top of the tree. "In Estella we have a great star; it is the star of our country. To some it means paradise. To others it means a place where insects cooperate together for a better life. To me it is the ideals of cooperation, kindness, and the eternal virtue of life." "Why are you here and not there?" Achilleas looked up at the stars. "I left to find myself, and I was confused by Vanusha for a moment, but now I can never return to Estella, for I am fallen from grace. I have failed all their ideals and ways. I am an outcast now. I have nowhere to go." Roxanne looked at Achilleas. "Did you find yourself?" "I found too late that I was an Estellan. Who am I but a fallen knight?" Achilleas looked at Roxanne. "Why do you watch these stars every night?" Roxanne looked up at the stars. "Each star is a dream. I choose a star and put a dream in that star. Each night I visit my dreams. They are only dreams. None will ever come true. This land is the place where dreams die. Not just dreams, everything dies. Vanusha controls all things; nothing happens without her consent, as you have learned. We are not free. My dreams can never be while Vanusha and her land of death persists." "Why do you avoid me in public?" Roxanne looked at Achilleas. "I am not allowed to be with you. You belong to Vanusha. She has chosen you. If she finds I have spoken to you, I will be punished." "I have not chosen Vanusha." "It is not yours to choose. She is the goddess; if she chooses you, you must yield to her advances or you will be destroyed." Achilleas frowned. "I do not choose Vanusha, I choose Roxanne." Roxanne smiled. "You would choose a hopeless dreamer over a goddess?" "My king told me when I left Estella to seek kindness. You are kindness. So I seek you." Roxanne shook her head. "Our love is just another hopeless dream. I will deposit it in a star and never be able to reach it." "Roxanne, one day you and I will take wing together and soar to the stars." Roxanne looked at Achilleas. "I thought

I was a dreamer. We must only dream, for the stars will forever be too far to fly to." Achilleas spent every night with her since that meeting. They would dream together and deposit each dream in a star. They would kiss and say, "Until we reach the stars."

Vanusha one day asked Achilleas to follow her. He did, and they traveled far from the oak. They crossed the lake and the wind was with them, so their flight had speed. Vanusha stopped at the top of an elm. She pointed. Achilleas looked where she pointed, and there was the great star hung on the three rocks. It was Estella. Vanusha said, "They are not protecting themselves from invasion. They post no guards; they are fools." Achilleas looked at Vanusha. "They do not expect enemies. They live in bliss." Vanusha smiled. "So much easier for us." Achilleas shook his head. "What do you mean?" Vanusha looked at the great star of Estella. "We will conquer these Estellans. They will look upon their star and see the power of Vanusha forever. They will be our slaves and we will rule the entire greater lake area. It is our destiny as wasps to rule all the other creatures. The sun put us here to be the power of death over all life." Achilleas swallowed his words and followed Vanusha back to the great oak tree on the other side of the lake. As darkness fell, Achilleas went to see Roxanne. The stars burned bright high in the oak. Achilleas looked at Roxanne. "I must leave. I must go warn the Estellans before Vanusha invades them." Roxanne moved close to Achilleas. "Will they listen to you?" "I hope so. I have to try. They are my friends." Roxanne looked up at the stars. "Will I ever see you again?" Achilleas pointed at a star. "The dream of together again will be in that star." Roxanne looked across at all the stars. "Wherever you are you will see the same stars, and that way we will always share the same dreams." "Yes, our dreams will live wheresoever we shall go." They said together, "Until we reach the stars." Then they kissed one last time and Achilleas disappeared into the night sky.

Achilleas flew toward the lake. The sky grew thunderous and the wind began to blow. He weathered against the wind, but the rain, too, began to fall, first in big drops, then like a waterfall. As it happened, Achilleas was over the lake at the time. His wings grew heavier and heavier until he could no longer keep aloft. He fell like a ball of lead into the lake. The waters were great waves that tossed his inert body around like a top. There was only darkness, and Achilleas heard a lady's voice. "There can only be one star." Achilleas gulped water. "But the heavens are full of stars." The lady said, "But there is room for only one star in your heart." Achilleas shook his head as water splashed over him. "Roxanne and I, we choose a star for every dream. I have found there are enough stars for every dream." The lady laughed. "There is only one dream for each soul. A dream of life, a dream of death, a dream of Estella, or even a dream of Vanusha. These are the dreams that fit each living soul." Achilleas sunk under a wave. "Who are you?." She laughed again. "The real question is, 'Who are you?'" Water splashed across Achilleas. "I am Achilleas, former knight of Estella, follower of the living goddess Vanusha, outcast from all lands. Who are you?" The waters went still suddenly. "I am the Lady of the Lake, mother of life and queen of the universe." Achilleas looked up and the moon shone through a veil of clouds. "Are you God?" The lady laughed. "God is never what you expect or anticipate. I am God. For God is wisdom. I am God. For God is love. This is not the only lake; there are many lakes, but more so the entire universe is a lake and I am its keeper. Does that answer your question?" Achilleas floated on the waters. "Why have you come to me?" "Because I had a question for you before I let you pass into the land of God." Achilleas looked up at the moon burning bright in the night sky. "What is that question?" "There are two stars in your life; which one do you choose? The star of King Rex or the star of the living goddess Vanusha? The conflict in your soul is obvious." Rex looked at his inert soaked wings and paddled to keep afloat. "But tell me if Rex's philosophy was correct—you are God after all." "Your friend was wise, but you must discover wisdom of your own accord. Who is your star, Rex or Vanusha?" Achilleas looked up at the moon. "Is this a test?" The lady laughed. "Your whole life has been a test; this is only the outcome of your life as you have lived it." Achilleas closed his eyes. "My choice is Rex." "Are you sure?" Achilleas opened one eye and nodded. "Yes, Estella will always be my star." The wind blew and the lake's waters rippled. "Then you must find your redemption in your star." "How can I be redeemed, for I have fallen so far from grace?" "In the light of that star, that Rex, that kingdom Estella is all the redemption you will ever need." The first light of day shone through the horizon. Just then a great caterpillar floating on a leaf fished Achilleas from the waters. Achilleas looked up at the caterpillar. "Is this the land of God?" The caterpillar took a twig and used it as a paddle in the calm morning waters of the lake. "Of course this is the land of God. I am Isadore, one of God's very own servants." The caterpillar smiled. "The lady has sent me to rescue you, so here I am." Achilleas shook his head. "You know of the lady?" "Of course I do. I work for her, ugly as I am." "Then you know she has sent me —" The caterpillar put his hand to Achilleas's mouth. "What the lady has told you is for you and you alone. It was not for my ears." Achilleas tried his wet wings, but they only spluttered. "I must get on my way to Estella. I have to warn them." The caterpillar hushed the great wasp. "You can go nowhere just this minute. Give it time, and you shall be all right." The leaf boat entered a calm harbor where wildflowers grew on the shore. The caterpillar carried the wasp onto the shore and deposited him beneath a group of yellow wildflowers. Isadore looked out to the lake. "This is my home, the most beautiful harbor in all the lake." The caterpillar stood on the lake's edge and looked at his reflection in the waters. "I serve such great beauty; what a shame that I am so ugly." Achilleas laid there in a heap. "You are no uglier than any other worm." Isadore looked at his reflection and sighed. "Ugliness, will you ever leave me?" Achilleas said under his breath. "You're not ugly . . ." The caterpillar brought some herbs to the wasp. "These herbs will help you convalesce." Achilleas chewed on the herbs. "Aren't you afraid of me? I'm one of your common predators."

Isadore laughed. "No. I do what the lady asks. No matter what it is. But healing I do for pleasure. I have helped many other creatures, some my predators, not just because the lady asks but because it is life's joy to give life. I was not born with a stinger or great venom or mighty mandibles. God gave me kindness as my only weapon. I can give life with my gathered knowledge. It is the lady's virtue to make life from life. That is how I became her servant." Achilleas nodded. "Now I know why she did what she did." He looked at Isadore. "She is leading me to life. She has been doing it all along." Isadore closed his eyes as he stood by the lake. Achilleas looked quizzically. "What are you doing?" Isadore smiled. "Quiet, I am praying." "What is a prayer?" Isadore opened his eyes. "A prayer is how your soul speaks to the lady. It is when her soul and yours are one." Achilleas looked at Isadore. "Can I pray with you?" The caterpillar nodded. "I shall lead us both. Close your eyes." Achilleas closed his eyes. Isadore also closed his eyes. "Our lady, look within our souls and find kindness as we look within yours and find everlasting love. We need thy presence in our lives, the guiding wind that leads us to the right and to the just and to the good. Protect us, protect our friends, protect all living beings. Fill our cups with your beauty, make us in your image kind and wise and righteous. Not so we become proud, but so we become humbled by the power of life to give life. Amen." Achilleas opened his eyes. "Thank you. I liked that." Isadore smiled. "Usually I pray quietly; it's nice to have company." Every day after, while Achilleas healed, they would pray together quietly with their eyes closed. But soon enough Achilleas was healed and his wings were ready for flight. However, there was something wrong with Isadore. He grew tired and weak. Achilleas would help him, and he knew he could not leave Isadore in such a condition. In his soul, he was torn between his friends in Estella and his new friend. He knew he had to reach and warn the Estellans soon, but he also knew he could not leave the person who saved his life and healed him to die in solitude. Achilleas stayed and helped his friend. One day Isadore sat down to pray. He was so tired and weak he could hardly stay upright. Isadore looked at his reflection. "I am so ugly, thank heaven soon my soul will rise in beauty from my tomb." Achilleas sat to pray with the caterpillar. "Don't talk that way. You will be better soon." They began to pray, and as they prayed Isadore began weaving a silk around his body. Soon he was surrounded by silk and was in a deep sleep. But Achilleas would not leave. He stayed to watch over his friend, though he could do nothing. After many days the caterpillar's silk turned dark and Achilleas could no longer see his friend. But the great wasp would sit and pray while he waited. Then one day the chrysalis cracked open and a butterfly awkwardly rose from the pupae tomb. Achilleas asked the butterfly, "Are you Isadore?" The butterfly said, "Isadore is a pretty name. Can I use it?" Achilleas smiled as he saw the butterfly's eyes were the same as the caterpillar's. "Your soul has risen from your tomb, Isadore. You are now beautiful forever." The butterfly flew off into the forest. "Isadore, you taught me how to pray. I shall never forget you." With that, Achilleas headed to Estella.

The great wasp fell prostrate before King Rex. "I am not worthy of this kingdom. I have hunted, I have eaten flesh. I have killed for pleasure. I am fallen. My fate is in your grasp." Rex raised his friend from the floor. "I told you long ago this lifestyle, this kingdom, is a choice. You choose to live with us because you will to do so, not because we command you. It is the way of freedom. What you did while you were not with us is not my affair, only what you do here in Estella is my business." Achilleas looked up at Rex. "I need you to redeem me." Rex smiled. "If forgiveness is what you want, I forgive you. But redemption is between you and the God inside. Only God can give you the redemption that will ever satisfy you." Rex pointed at his chest. "God is inside; ask God and she shall redeem you." Achilleas stood upright. "God told me to seek redemption in you." Rex looked at Achilleas. "I have forgiven you all that I can. Seek inside yourself for the rest."

Achilleas looked away. "There is more. The wasp land that I lived in has become determined in its quest to conquer Estella." Rex looked at Achilleas. "We shall prepare our defenses. Now go and find your redemption and we shall talk more." Achilleas returned to the safe harbor where Isadore once lived. Here the great wasp sat before the lake to pray. "Great lady of this lake, please guide me to my redemption." The sun began to sink into the horizon. The moon rose up into the painted sky. "My dear poor Achilleas, did Rex not forgive you?" Achilleas opened his eyes and looked up at the moon. "King Rex forgave me, but it was not enough." The darkness swallowed the last beams of daylight and fireflies began to dance in the moonlight. "You seek my forgiveness, but even that will not be enough. You need to forgive yourself. The power of forgiveness starts with you, not with a great king or even a mighty goddess. Redemption is inside you. It always was." Achilleas looked out toward the windy lake. "I cannot forgive myself; I have done wrong, and it is a stain that will never wash." The moon lit the night with its light. "Do you, Achilleas, forgive me, the Lady of the Lake? For you were in my care, and it was I that failed you. I am that voice inside, and at every turn I could have changed your course." Achilleas shook his head. "I can forgive you, my lady, you are God. It was not your fault, it was only a mistake." "Achilleas, you had no fault either; it was only a mistake." Achilleas looked up at the moon. "Deliver me from this sin." "Deliver yourself and you will be redeemed. After all, why pray for what you can give yourself?" Achilleas looked out across the lake. "Is it that simple?" "Find it in your soul, and it is that simple." "Then I am redeemed! My sin is gone!" The night sky was filled with the dancing fireflies like a thousand stars in the sky. "You are home in Estella again. It was when you redeemed yourself that you could finally return home." The fireflies lit up in the shape of a star. "There can only be one star," said the lady. Achilleas smiled. "Yes, it's time to ensure that forevermore."

King Rex brought together a council of war. Achilleas stood before the great spider. "Rex, it is not enough to sit here and wait. The best defense is a good offense. If we wait for them to come here we will put Estellans in jeopardy. I propose we assault them at their home so we won't have to fight in our own home." Rex smiled. "That is precisely what I thought. But you are hiding something in your reasoning, Achilleas." The wasp looked at the king. "Yes, I have a female wasp I want to rescue, but that is not the only reason for wanting to attack them at their home." Rex laughed. "We will most certainly move mountains to rescue your love, Achilleas. This kingdom is in your debt many times over. That is as good a reason as any other." Achilleas looked down. "Nothing for me, Rex, everything for Estella." Rex looked at Queen Estella. "He who wants nothing for himself will always deserve everything." Queen Estella smiled. "We are a kingdom of romantics; we would move every asset to preserve love in this world." Rex looked at Achilleas. "Love is our reason for being a kingdom. Love is what has brought all of us together. Love is the wind that blows Estella's sails. Love is the only and best reason for doing anything in life."

They prepared the siege of the Vanushans. The king's architect, the ant Flavius, put it all in motion. It was all so far away across the lake. Easy if you can fly, but only a part of Estella's army was aerial. Plus you had to supply an army. Which was my job as head of the king's logistical command. I worked very closely with the genius Flavius. He had created a way to move troops and supplies together quickly. This was what he called the ant wheel. Ants would lock arms and legs together up and around until the circle closed. By shifting their weight, the ants would roll in a big wheel. This gave greater speed and a shock value that was awesome. Flavius learned to do this from counting. He had studied how counting and natural phenomena worked together. Ants count constantly and are always building. It seemed like an observation only an ant could make. To cross the lake, Flavius decided to build a bridge. This was no ordinary bridge it was a bridge of ants one interlocked within the other. To do so he would carry ants on butterflies to the opposite side. Another of his inventions called the bent leaf would be used as a sail to bring ants to the ground instead of landing the butterflies. This meant that the butterflies could unload ants en route and return quickly to reload. It was all very efficient as well as safe, because spiders were hidden in the brush to protect the bridge ants. The bridge grew from both ends of the lake and met in the middle. It took a little doing, but quickly the bridge was built and wheels crossed carrying spiders, ant majors, and supplies. One of those wheels carried Rex and me. Once the wheels got rolling, they carried across the bridge and rolled furiously to the great oak of Vanusha. There they all stopped. Rex stood before the mighty host and looked up toward the tree. "Today is the battle of our lives. Our enemies are intent to spread death to the ends of the earth. All we have is the virtue of life. It is our only shield. Tonight there will be only one victor. It is either life or death. One will be vanquished. Never to play its play on this stage again. All the hopes of life go with us. This kingdom Estella has lived as an example of our virtue. We will win not because we are better, but because the virtue of life fires our blood. Mercy be our guide, for life is our goal, and though death is all around, may life benefit our virtue today. We are an example of all that is good, all that is right. By our example we challenge others to live better. Let not our example perish from this earth. We shall live up to our legacy if we act by the mercy of God to win this day, not just for us but for all insects!"

The plan was to send the wasps in after the Vanushans first, then fly spiders to the top of the tree in the second move by way of butterflies. Then the main army was to go up the tree and finish the battle. Rex moved with the spiders to the top of the oak while Achilleas and the wasps engaged the Vanushans in a chase that was meant to draw the Vanushan main attack away from the tree. Rex and the spiders found little resistance high up in the oak as almost all Vanushans engaged the wasps of Estella. Achilleas and the Estellans drew the Vanushans into the woods. Then he turned to make his stand and just then, from behind the Vanushans, was an enormous host of Estellan wasps. The Vanushans, realizing they were surrounded, surrendered. Rex was met high in the tree by Roxanne. "Mercy on our goddess." Rex looked at her and smiled. "I am Rex; you need not beg for her mercy. I will not harm her." Then an imperious voice rang from above. "You may not harm me, but I shall harm you indeed!" Vanusha appeared hovering over Rex. "We meet at last," said Rex. "You and your kingdom are an abomination," said Vanusha. "Likewise could be said about Vanushans," Rex laughed. They stood there in the high tree the sun shone through, and one could see a spider floating on light and a wasp that was shining brightly. Vanusha began to stare into Rex's eyes. Rex became transfixed, and her deadly tail was about to move when out came a scream. "Rex! Look out!" said Achilleas. In an instant, Rex spit silk and blinded Vanusha. In the next instant, Achilleas speared Vanusha on his stinger. That was the end of the Vanushans forevermore. Achilleas returned to Estella with the beautiful Roxanne, where they would sit at night watching the stars and both say, "We have reached the stars." Then they would kiss.

Achilleas and Roxanne lived for many years in the kingdom Estella and also had a child.

Of the many tales of Estella, this one of a knight lost and redeemed is one of great passion for me. For there is only one star: the star of Estella, that will burn forever bright.

Return of the White Spider

The chronicles of Rodney Roach, volume three. Once upon a dream there was a great kingdom called Estella. It was so long ago. It was a place where insects cooperated to their betterment. Where the strong protected the weak. Where the ideals of King Rex replaced the thoughtless barbarism that was before. But that is all gone now. Nothing remains except for the dream. Dreams and memories live in the darkness, and by moonlight you believe they are a treasure beyond summation. But hold it in the hand at sunrise and the air heats up and the light fills the void and every dream and memory has vanished from existence. The last memories of the kingdom were ugly as the nation itself was beautiful. King Rex, on his deathbed, had declared that only the wisest would succeed him. This set the kingdom ablaze with ambition. Who can measure who is wiser than the next? Not I. Not anybody. Factions formed, sides were chosen, and a civil war ensued.

Who was to stop it? Queen Estella, for whom the kingdom was named, died just after Rex from her sorrow and longing. Achilleas, the first knight of the realm, would not choose sides, so his wife and son were murdered. He became a hermit living on the far side of the lake. Flavius, the king's architect, ran far away before any harm could come to him and his family. It doesn't matter who did what to whom. What matters is the kingdom fell, and fell hard. The infighting left no army to protect the citadel. Others filled the vacuum, such as the spider King Diomededs and the praying mantis King Rufio. They devoured what was left of Estella and then proceeded to fight each other in a long, long war. Finally a treaty was signed between the predators to share the predation. Good if you were spider or mantis. All others were just food for the mighty. Darkness ruled the land. Hope was a secret. Those of us that still dreamed gathered in secret places. All we had was our faded memory of a dream. I was the head of this secret society. The Shining Star was what we called it. Rex had asked me to keep the flames of the dream lit, and I did just that. Shining Star was the last drop of hope in a vast desert of sorrow. Freedom is a shining star that is in the distance and seems unreachable, yet is within your grasp and your dreams. It takes courage, perseverance, and an unwillingness to give up. Each day we would say to each other, "Me too in Estella." This was our deepest wish and also how we greeted each other. We had hidden in our secret place that famous star of Estella, which we venerated like a relic from God himself. We had little hope of any future until he was born. A member of the society, the cricket Archibald was a watcher of stars in the sky, and he said that a new star was in the sky brighter than the others. It was believed among us that this shining star was prophetic. "Could it be?" we would ask. "Could the king be returning this time with all the power of heaven?" And so it came to pass that a white spider was born to the mother spider Soraya. It was under that prophetic star. Nothing happened the way we expected it would happen. We convened a special council at the Shining Star. At the entrance of our hidden tree we heard a thump. The person said, "Me too in Estella." It was Queen Miranda and her daughter Frances. They were praying mantises and defied the orders of her husband, the king, to avoid the abomination of Estella. But there they were in our secret of secrets, challenging all the fates with the rest of us. I was the moderator of this event. "The prophetic child has been born to the spider Soraya. From all accounts he is a white spider with transparent legs. The problem remains that spider King Diomedes and the mantis King Rufio have made a law that all white spiders will be killed upon birth. We must get the spider to safety prior to the kings taking action. Are there any ideas from the society?"

The mantis Queen Miranda spoke. "This is of grave danger, as my husband and Diomedes are already sending soldiers to capture or kill the young white spider. It would take a great warrior to save him. I will do what I can to delay the situation." Miranda's daughter Frances whispered in her mother's ear. "My daughter said we will fight to the last for this young king, and I believe it just may come down to that." Archibald the cricket spoke up. "We could all arm ourselves and fight." I said, "We are no match as a group against these mantis and spider armies. There is only one creature that can help us . . . Achilleas." The ant Desimunde spoke up. "Nobody has seen Achilleas since the fall of Estella." "I know where he is, I just need a ride there. It's the only hope we have." We made our plans then and there. I would find Achilleas and everyone else would delay the execution until the great wasp could intervene in our favor. Elsa the butterfly flew me across the lake. The wind blew with us and it took us less time than usual. I looked for the place that Achilleas so often described: golden wildflowers by a pretty little harbor. There he was, praying by the lakeshore. The butterfly hovered above him. The great wasp was in a deep reverie. "Achilleas," I said. "Yes, my lady," said Achilleas. I rolled my eyes. "Achilleas! It's me, Rodney Roach!" Achilleas opened his eyes. "Rodney, what brings you to this distant place?" "I need your help." "They destroyed everything I loved over succession. I have no more to give." The butterfly Elsa landed. "The old kingdom is gone, but we have a chance for a new one." Achilleas shook his head. "Did you finally discover who was the wisest?" "Nobody shall ever be as wise as Rex. That is what I mean. What if King Rex returned?" Achilleas looked up at the sky. "That is impossible." "How about a white spider with transparent legs born under a prophetic star? Still impossible?" "I must pray to understand what I will do." "We haven't any time for prayer." "I must pray." In the meantime, the mantis and spider soldiers were making their way to the lair of the spider Soraya. Desimunde and Archibald prepared an armed reception party for the coming soldiers. They came armed with sharp sticks and lots of courage. Desimunde was at the front, holding his stick. Archibald was at the back, claiming he would be the last to fall. The mantis and spider soldiers met the small party at a bottleneck in the road to the white spider. Desimunde looked at the soldiers and screamed, "May the song of our winter be the spring for Estella." With that he charged the soldiers. Desimunde was the first to fall.

They fought with all the fury of those who have nothing to lose. They were defeated, but Archibald was the last to fall, and as he did he screamed, "Heaven's star is made mortal. You cannot kill him—he is beyond your ways." They ran him over and left him for dead. But Archibald lived, and it is from him that I know this story. Archibald followed the soldiers to the lair of the spider Soraya. the young white spider named Frank was with his mother as she was about to feed him. The soldiers went forward. "Spider Soraya, you will accompany us to see the kings. They will decide what to do with you." With that, Soraya and her child left their home and went to see the kings. Diomedes was on a dais. Rufio talked to his wife and child. Soraya and Frank entered the hall of kings. Rufio quickly went up on the dais and to his throne. Diomedes the spider king spoke first. "White spider, you are an anomaly among spiders. Your color is the antithesis of what is correct." Rufio the mantis king broke in. "Yes. One look at him and all the propaganda about Estella is made manifest. Those who yearn for this abomination only draw hope when they see this ugly creature." Soraya looked up at the kings. "What are your intensions with my son, oh great kings?" Diomedes began to laugh. "We intend to kill him. This wretch will not fire any revolutions in our kingdom." Soraya stood on her back legs, making herself look larger. "I will not let you kill my son." Suddenly the mantis Queen Miranda stood beside Soraya. "I will not let you kill him either." Suddenly the young mantis Princess Frances stood before Soraya and her mother. "I will not let you kill him either." Miranda looked at Rufio, her husband. "Estella is our future, not this abomination." Rufio screamed, "Traitors! You have breathed too long in this kingdom. You have filled my child with evil stories of an illegitimate place. Now I will destroy the lot of you." Diomedes moved forward and yelled to his soldiers, "Surround and destroy!" The soldiers surrounded Soraya, Frank, Miranda, and Frances. Soraya and Miranda both stepped forward and attacked the soldiers. Soraya fought like this was the last stand, and it was for her. Miranda lasted longer and fought with great precision. But the mantis and spider soldiers were too much for them. This was the end—Soraya dead and Miranda severely wounded. The spider and mantis soldiers moved in on the children. Miranda swiftly got the children beneath her. One last spider bite and she fell dead. The children Frank and Frances were all alone.

The soldiers now moved in on the children. Both children stood crying over their dead mothers beneath them. Frances turned to Frank and said, "Are you scared?" Frank answered, "Yes. Very scared." Just then the hum of wings pierced the air and a great wasp warrior entered the hall. Riding atop Elsa the butterfly came Rodney Roach. Achilleas swept the children up in his appendages and he carried them to safety. Rodney then gathered the children and rode them off on Elsa the butterfly, while Achilleas fought the oncoming soldiers and dispatched them easily. Then, when the butterfly was airborne with Rodney and the children, the great warrior wasp made an exit with the butterfly. They flew to the far side of the lake, to a beautiful little harbor full of yellow flowers. That was how it all began—full of just-in-times, full of tragedy, and still full of hope.

To live in exile is like standing at the farthest point from a nourishing light. You feel the warmth as an absence of cold. The light is also the very absence of darkness. It is your distant dream. It is your heaven . . . and the siege of heaven is your daily ambition. We were all exiles from Estella, and that light was at a very great distance. But hope lay in the light of children's eyes. Frank was very, reserved and it was to be expected after his ordeal.

Frances was more open and jovial. She apparently had faced the ordeal with advance judgment. First thing was to teach them the vegetarian way. I would gather the food and Achilleas would show them the reason for eating this way. I would say, "They'll never learn." Achilleas would look at the children. "We do not kill in order to stay alive. We do this by choice. Nobody forces us to do this. Eating must nourish without killing. It is the power of life giving life. We must preserve life and only eat food that preserves others' lives." Frank raised his hand. "Are you saying that fruit and grain are not alive?"

Achilleas thought a moment. "Not autonomous and thinking like us. The kind of life worth preserving is like us. It thinks, moves, breathes. It is capable of the deepest emotion and the most profound works of philosophy." Frances asked, "Which nourishes us more, eating fruits and grains or eating a prey we hunt?" Frank smiled. I answered for Achilleas. "You are nourished more by the prey you hunt, but that is not the point. Your body may be nourished more but your soul is left to starve. Your soul is only nourished by the kindness of your actions, by the goodness of your purpose." Achilleas interrupted. "It is by the purpose of life giving life that you nourish your soul the most. We hunted by necessity, but no necessity declares our need for life giving life—only the call of our souls for the purpose of enriching our spirit. We are not just flesh that needs to feed on flesh, we are souls seeking the nourishment of kindness to profit our tender flame. Gentleness is the heart of our philosophy. King Rex used to say, 'Be kind to strangers; a kindness given is a kindness received.' We are gentle warriors filled with the compassion of God. If we must fight we will, but as Rex would say, we seek kindness, not conquest. Rex was very wise; he was the heart and reason for the existence of our kingdom, Estella. Nothing has been the same without him." Achilleas looked at Frank. "We hope he will return one day." Frances smiled. "Tell us about the cooperation." I, Rodney, looked at Frances. "You already seem to know. Why don't you tell it?" Frances looked at Frank. "In Estella the people did not argue with each other or hunt each other. They all cooperated. Those with the nose for grain and fruit would harvest them, and those with strength would protect the others." Achilleas looked at Frank and Frances. "We protected the weak and the weak protected us by nourishing us with vegetarian foods. Rather than hunt the weak we protected them. This is very important. The strong must protect the weak; it is their higher calling. Creatures that protect the weak are nourished by the kindness of their actions and ennobled by the virtue of their cause." I, Rodney, interrupted my friend. "You see, virtue is our real food—it is the lictor that flows in our veins. The real work in this world is the work of the spirit. We daily build the architecture of our soul, and the brick and mortar of our spirit is kindness." Achilleas looked sternly at the kids with his antennae back. "What you do in life will determine the strength of your spirit, the richness of your soul. The lady of the lake, which is God, will call you to heaven if you have been a creature of kindness and end you then and there if you are not. But our purpose cannot be to get into heaven but to do kindness for the sake of kindness. We are the stuff of possibilities if only we find a gentle path towards our ends. No amount of belief will get you there, only the knowledge that your goodness of spirit is defined by the kindness of your actions." Our lectures would end only to begin again. Time passed, and you could see how the children looked up to Achilleas. They learned to pray and would ask questions about prayer and God. Quizzically, Frank asked, "What is God?" Achilleas looked out toward the lake. "She is the lady of the lake. This is not her only lake; in fact, the entire universe is her lake."

"She is beauty and kindness. She counts your actions and will help you along the way if you are good of spirit. God is outside and within as well. She brings together all things and also breaks them asunder. Pray to her and you shall see." Prayed to her we did. Together, as the sun would set, we would all sit together and pray. The children seemed to like this time the best. Frank was more animated when in prayer than when doing anything else.

Time passed and the children grew older. One day by the lake Frank was playing. He would look into the lake and see his own reflection, then he would duck and hide so his reflection couldn't see him back. He kept doing this over and over again. Then he heard the lady's voice calling him to stop. Then the lady's voice told him, "Look into your reflection; do not avoid it." So Frank looked into his reflection. What he saw was a white spider with transparent legs looking back at him. "Who are you?" Frank said. The reflection answered back, "I am King Rex." Frank said, "How can it be you? You are dead." The reflection answered back, "I am dead. But the lady of the lake is allowing me to speak with you through our reflections. It is important that I speak with you." Frank looked at Rex. "What do you want?" Rex smiled. "You and I look so much alike and the situation is so desperate. There is only you to carry on my legacy. I see in you the son I never had. I need you to take on the injustice in the world. You are young and you don't yet understand the meaning of Estella. It was a place where all insects could value life. Where we were free and in our freedom liberated to do any wonder our minds aspired to. Long have insects suffered dreaming of a place worthy of their daylight dreams. Where food was plentiful and all cooperated for the greater good."

"It is possible, for we lived it if only for a brief period of time." Frank looked earnestly at Rex. "What do you want from me?" Rex thought a moment. "I want you to grow up and be ready for a great struggle. To put everything you are into bringing back Estella. You must learn to be like me." Frank was upset. "But I don't want to be like you. I want to be myself." "No, that is not what I mean." Frank began to cry. "I will never be like you. I will never be you. Nothing in me signals that desire. All I shall ever be is me!" With that Frank ran from the lip of the lake. He screamed, "I will never be another Rex! Not ever!!" Achilleas was visibly disappointed. I sat by my great friend and I cried. A dream was ending and we were unable to stop it from dying. All we had struggled for was gone.

Time passed. Frank would avoid his reflection as if hiding from the mask of death. Frances could not convince him that King Rex did not mean for him to give up his identity. The cicadas came as the leaves began to fall. They were noisy but wise. Winter would come soon, but the happy time in the sun with the cicadas was one we would remember, if only because it took us away from the stark realization that Frank would never be another Rex. One wise cicada named Rupert heard the story of how Frank refused to be the next Rex. "Do you know we cicadas live in the trees for seventeen years sucking juice from the wood? That is a long time to spend as a child. It is longer than most lives. We are only larvae then. Larvae life as a child is all we know. Then after seventeen long years we change into adults, and though our childhood notions were strongly embedded after seventeen years, we are different in every way. Our adult life hardly reflects our childhood." I looked at Rupert. "So what are you saying?" Rupert buzzed and said, "Young Frank is still a child; as he grows into an adult spider he will change his ideas. Life changes us all. The only thing we can sometimes count on is change." Time passed. The winter blew in cold and all the cicadas were dead. Change was all victorious. It was on a warm day in the beginning of winter that we faced the gravest challenge yet. It was like every other day. Achilleas was off to reconnaissance the surrounding area. He would check for danger. He didn't have to go far. Waiting for Achilleas to take flight was a robber fly. It is a deadly wasp predator. It was totally unexpected. With all the beauty of the lake that surrounded us, there was also the cold breath of death lurking in the shadows. Achilleas was very fast, but still the robber fly was faster. As robber flies do, this one grabbed onto its prey with spines that exist between its legs. The spines dug into Achilleas. The robber fly has a neurotoxin venom in his bite, and his jaws were coming nearer and nearer. Just in the nick of time Achilleas broke free from some of the spines, and he whipped around his thorax and impaled the robber fly on his stinger. The robber fly and Achilleas fell down to the ground and out of sight. Just then Francis turned to Frank. "Are you scared?" Frank responded, "Yes, I'm very scared."

Achilleas rose up from the ground and the robber fly was dead. But Achilleas quickly came crashing to the ground. We went over to him in a hurry. He was severely wounded. It was about to storm, so we dragged his body into the hollow of a tree. He looked at us all and said, "I am living in this moment. Maybe my last moment. It is too easy to be seduced by yesterday, and tomorrow may never come at all. I see my life through the prism of this moment. I dreamed with all my soul. But this moment is failure. All I have lived for is a new Estella that will not be. My last gasp is the knowledge that it could never be. The lady is coming for me . . . Please, please make it real again. Don't make the dream vanish before my very eyes. Like the fading flame of a forest fire, my dream glows fiercely only to be blown out by the perfidy of life and carried on the wind into oblivion. My lady, why make us aspire to something great only to extinguish it? Estella was the place where we all lived a waking dream. But was it only a dream. Was there nothing real to establish our futures upon? I lived to see it rise from simple ideas of a wise spider to a mighty kingdom set on values which its inhabitants could live by. I saw it fall after his death and fall and fall and fall. There is nothing left now, only the memory of what once was. The lady is here . . ." A clap of thunder punctuated his last words as Achilleas the mighty wasp was dead. The children cried and cried, but there was no reviving Achilleas; he was gone forever. The children were now full-grown adults. But they were struck hard by their mentor's death. Achilleas had looked after them for longer than their mothers had.

He was the world for the children. None took his death harder than Frank. For days after he was quiet and despondent. Frank went down to the lake and he began to look for his reflection. But nothing responded. He began to cry. "I abandoned Achilleas, and now Rex has abandoned me. I have failed everybody! I do not deserve to live." I tried to console him but nothing helped. I told him, "If you are ready for the burden of being our white spider, then Rex will appear. Nobody has abandoned anybody!" That very night a mist rose from the lake. Frank went by the lake, despondent. He was lost in his misery when he heard a voice. "Frank, do not lose your hope. I am here with you." Frank looked around and saw only mist. "Where are you?" Frank said. "The voice said, "I am a reflection in the mist. It's what makes a white spider most." "Rex?" "Yes, Frank, it is Rex and I am here to help you." "Achilleas is dead—there is no hope. I cannot do it alone." "You are not alone, Frank. Achilleas is here with me. We will do it together." "Achilleas is there with you?" "Yes, we are not abandoning you; we will help in our way to make you be the spider you need to be. Achilleas says that you have it in you; you always did." Frank smiled.

"What must I learn to succeed?" "You must learn to trust yourself. Believe in yourself. I did not do what I did by not being my own best advocate. You must be your own strength." "You can't help me?" "We will be there when you need us most. But we are just reflections of what you are. Like this mist, we are just a cloud that vanishes in the sunlight. You are the strength. You are who must do what must be done." Frank looked at the mist around him. "How can I become more like you?" "Frank, we are only reflections of each other. You must be the best you to succeed. It is not in being me that will make you the kind of person necessary for this task. Frank and Frank alone is necessary for this adventure." Frank looked down.

"How can I be sure that I will meet my destiny?" "Only the lady knows your destiny. Do not think of destiny. Think of the moment. Make the most out of the moment you are given. No spider has a destiny; we only make the moment worth remembering." Frank nodded. "How will I convince others to follow me?" "They only have to see you to want to follow you. You are the white spider. Now what you do once they want to follow you is harder. You must make a connection with them, a lasting bond. You must lead by your wits and always do what is just and right." Frank said, "How do I do that?" "Be true to yourself and think about what you do before you do it." "Is it that easy?" "Nothing is easy, but you will find your way. Always believe in yourself. Not just when it is easy, but when it is so hard you feel you want to hide. I leave you with these last words. Frank, never give up. Every step of the way you are here because nobody gave up on you. Your path is a hard one; do not expect it to be easy. You will have to defeat an evil and powerful foe. Do not underestimate them. They did not get where they are because they are fools. You must outwit them, and if you cannot, put your faith in the power of a dream. Dreams are powerful—they ignite the spirit and bring people together. Dream with them, not separate from them. In every insect's dream is a window to the future; build a path to that dream and you cannot fail."

"So long, Frank, the lady is with you. Bye." The mist began to dissipate and Frank returned to the tree. The next morning Frank stood at the entrance of the tree. Francis walked up to him. "Something on your mind?" she said. Frank looked at the morning light play on the golden flowers of the nook. "I'm thinking how hard the path ahead is and how you and Rodney may need to stay behind." "I thought we were in this together." "Don't you understand? You guys are my family and I don't want to see you hurt." Frances looked at me. "He thinks he doesn't need us." I looked at Frank. "Where are you going to go when you leave here?" Frank looked at me. "I thought I would head to the place where Estella once was and convince people to come to my side." I shook my roach head. "They will kill you before you accomplish anything. You can't walk in looking like that. You need a disguise." Frances brightened up. "You need to go to the Shining Star Society and have people come to you. It's the right place to hatch a revolution." I patted Frank on the back. "You need us to help you. Three minds are better than one." "Okay. Okay. I can see I will not make it without you." We cheered. And it was not long before we were on our way back to the Shining Star Society. We would follow the lip of the lake back. Francis would fly ahead and look out for danger. There was some red clay on the way. So we covered Frank completely with the red clay until we had made a white spider red. The distance was long and it took us many, many days, but before too long we were at the Shining Star Society. It was a secret place and we came upon it quietly.

The Shining Star Society seemed abandoned, as though it had been left in peace for centuries. As I entered cautiously I said what I had always said when crossing that threshold: "Me too in Estella." I heard a fearful, almost quiet voice say the same in return. "Me too in Estella." Then I saw Archibald come out of his hiding place. We hugged each other as good old friends do. Archibald said, "I thought you were dead. The rumor was that you all died. You don't know how cruel Rufio and Diomedes have been. They kill everything and ask no questions. It is worse now than it has ever been." I looked at Frank and he whispered, "Don't tell him now." So I said, "Do they still meet here?" Archibald sighed. "Not for a very long time. But I can spread the word and we can hold meetings again now that you are back." I said, "Yes, that would be good." Archibald looked at Frank and Frances quizzically. "And who are these persons?" "The mantis is Princess Frances and the spider is . . ." Frank beamed his eyes at me. "This is Serlio the red spider. He comes from far away to help us." I looked around for it but I did not see it. "Where is the star?" Archibald smiled and went over to the corner and pulled something from between the leaves. The evening light shone on the star and it glowed. "Rex's star—it is the only symbol we have of Estella. We may have lost Estella to the past, but the dream breathes and lives today. So long as we dream, then Estella lives."

Dreams are unusual things created by the lady to bring us closer to her. Dreams do not die, they live in the hopes of desperate people. When they seem lost it takes only a small reminder to kindle those fires and the dream comes raging back to life. They came to meet once again at the Shining Star Society—so many that the room could hardly fit them. Knowing the danger, they still came. In their vanishing hopes was a determination to overcome fear and clutch a dream they all held dear. Standing on the dais were I, the star, and Frank, the red spider. I spoke to the gathered. "This star was Rex's star. It is the only surviving relic from Estella. I was there with Rex from the beginning before there was an Estella. Before there was a dream. There were some roaches who lived with a vegetarian spider. They dreamt of nothing more than their next meal. It was a good life. But all things change. Estella came and went in our history. But it was there, and oh, what a place to remember. I am not here today to tell you about the past of Estella but of the future of Estella . . . Archibald?" I said, looking toward Archibald. Archibald brought some water on a leaf. Frank began washing off the red clay and, as quick as could be, a red spider turned white. Archibald spoke up. "Oh, that is the secret." The audience grew loud with "Ahs." You could see the light reflecting through the white spider and the spider web star at the same time. The crowd began to kneel before the white spider. I gestured to Frank to speak. Frank spoke. "I am here to lead you out of tyranny." The crowd broke out in cheers. "I want you to know that I am not only your leader, but I am a seeker of the dream just like you. Me too in Estella." The crowd cheered again. Then the crowd spoke in unison. "Me too in Estella." Plans were made and the crowd was sent to gather friends for the inevitable fight. They were still afraid, but now they had something to fight for.

Courage is difficult to come by in a world where your life has no value. It's far easier to sit back and hide from the oncoming danger. Those that lived in the kingdom of Rufio and Diomedes did not sit back; they gathered what courage they had and made their way to the knotted tree, which was to be the place where the battle would take place. They came with what they had: a determination to live in a place where they could be of value. Many came, but as expected, it was not enough, for a far vaster army was fielded by Rufio and Diomedes. On the field beneath the knotted tree, the small army of Frank's was dwarfed

and surrounded by that of Rufio and Diomedes. The
leaders of both sides came out to meet on the field. There
were Rufio, Diomedes, Frank, and Francis. Diomedes
spoke first. "So you are the white spider. You think there is
some magic in being a white spider that your very
presence will win the day. You have made a grave error.
What will win this day is superior military capability. My
men are trained, and they are all predators, while your
army is a rabble of crickets, roaches, and sundry insects.
You do not stand a chance."

Frank spoke back. "We may not be professional like
you, but we make up for it in spirit and determination."
Francis looked at her father. "Father, you will lose this day
and I will avenge my mother." Rufio answered, "You
should have never come back." Frank looked at the army
of Diomedes and Rufio. "We are finished talking. When
next we meet it will be in battle." They finished and each
side returned to their army. Frank stood before his army
and he spoke to them. "It was a hard path to this point. I
have lost family and friends. Today I face the greatest
challenge of my life. We live here, we die here by our own
hand. This is not random; we are acting on our will. By
that will and that will alone hangs our fortunes. Give up
on destiny. There is only this moment. And in this
moment we have fortune on our side, for our wills are
strong and our determination is fortified. Nothing can
beat you if you believe you can do it. Think of the
kingdom you are leaving. It is the kingdom of death. We
were all already dead, so we have nothing to lose. Estella is
tomorrow. Today is the land of the dead, and we are
already dead, therefore we are invincible. Live the
moment. Me too in Estella!" Frank looked up at the

knotted tree and perceived a mist begin to obscure the vision. Frank said under his breath, "Rex." The mist rolled in quickly and soon there was almost nothing that could be seen. In those conditions Frank gave the order to attack. The armies met in the blind white environment that was suddenly to the advantage of Frank's army. Battles are a controlled storm. The front of the Rufio and Diomedes army was like a wave of bodies that mowed forward over the smaller Frank army. That is, until the chaos of the white blindness set in. Then the solid wave turned to whirlpools of activity. The chaos was what ruled the day, not the steady wall of military force.

In the wild mess that was this battle, Frances looked for Frank. She was wounded but not severely. She looked through the twisted chaos of bodies. The battle was ending and we would soon know the victors. Through bodies twisted up like the knotted tree, she saw the body of the white spider. She went to him instantly. She helped him up. He was still alive. "Frank . . . Frank . . . my love." Frank opened his eyes. "Did you say 'my love'?" Frances nodded. "Yes, you are my love and have been since before I met you." "You just have always been there, and I know in my soul that you are the one I love." Frances smiled. "Yes, I know." Frank smiled. "Was I that obvious?" "Yes, you were. Now let's try and get you off the ground." Francis helped Frank off the ground. Frank grimaced. "I can't move my back legs." Something else caught Francis's attention. "Do you hear that?" "What?" said Frank. Frances looked into the distance that was occluded by mist. "There is an army approaching, and by the sound of it, it is an army of spiders." Frank sighed. "That is the end." Frances moved closer to Frank. "Are you afraid?"

"Yes, very afraid." The mist began to lift. Frank looked at the lifting mist and shook his head. "Even Rex can help us no more." A whisper on the mist caught Frank's ear. "Do not give up." And as the mist melted away the sun broke through and the marching spiders came alive with a light of their own. For those spiders on the front line each carried a star made from web, and that star signified Estella. The spiders finished off the remnants of Rufio and Diomedes's army.

Rufio and Diomedes were also dead. The battle was over and Estella would have its day again.

The battle done, Frank and Frances spoke to the victorious army beneath the knotted tree.

Frank spoke first. "This is your day. I share it with you. It was not a white spider that was the difference. You yourselves are the difference. You are Estella much more than a white spider. And when you put your children to bed you should tell them how a white spider did come to lead you, but it was ordinary insects that made the difference. Estella cannot be built on a white spider alone. What builds Estella is you. We will pass on into the lady's realm, but you will remain. The kingdom will flourish with or without a white spider. It is your responsibility to make it so." Then Frances spoke. "What can we build now but another Estella? But has Estella really left us? It is in each and every one of our hearts. We are all here because Estella never left us, and we must live our lives in the way taught to us by the great King Rex. In those gentle ways we shall find our path back to our home. Me too in Estella." Frank repeated her words. "Me too in Estella." The crowd cheered. Frank and Francis would be King Frank and Queen Francis. Estella would return as would cooperation, defense of the weak, and above all, kindness. If there is more to tell I will not know. I am very old now. I have seen the coming of a kingdom, its fall, and its return. The lady holds nothing more in my destiny than as scribe to a great story. The lady is coming for me. Perhaps muster one last word . . . STAR.

POETRY

STARS

Stars
In the heart of a rose lay a great black hole.
The petals spread like the arms of a spiral galaxy.
There in the pulsing soul of the universe I found your reflection like drops of water on a pond.
From the pitch black of heaven I cut you a dress.
The stars cling to the cloth and because of the curvature of time it fits snug to the hips.
For eye color I choose the luminous tail of a comet.
From nebulae I make you nylons.
For your hair I construct a comb of quasars.

From the crimson light of a red dwarf I make paint
to adorn your lips.

I look for the most empty point in space and with
that inky darkness I line your eyes.

From pearlescent planets I make you earrings.

And sewing the asteroid belt through the rings of
Saturn I make a necklace.

You are at last dressed to the nines, clad by the sky.

The cosmos is a perfect fit.

The stars are shinning in your eyes.

I hear the ripples on the pond call your name.

In my guilded garden I bent to smell a rose.

I closed my eyes and the memory of the stars is
imprinted on my soul.

Like the kiss of a blackhole it draws me back to the
universe in your eye.

BEAUTY

Beauty
You are the answer to every question of my soul.
The ending to all the beginnings in my heart,
the last desperate spark that lights my solitary flame
in the midnight black,
and when at last the magnets of our proximity have
us touch,
the winds of Eden fill my being,
our kiss becomes the seal of god.

MIDNIGHT

Midnight

The moon shines on your face,
Beautiful stars are in your eyes.
Your golden hair is glimmering in the fairy light.
It is midnight and your kiss is a pomegranate on my lips.
I can smell angel lilies in the air.
The shadows of twisted trees stand all around.
Dawn can not exist at the darkest hour of the night.
Pale blue eyes like mid day skies.
Your smile ignites my heart with the magic of midnight rainbows.
Could we be just phantoms that meet at the darkest time
To enjoy one moment sublime?
When we sleep the prison of our bodies is unlocked
And we wander the nocturnal landscape in search of a place to call home.
Once found the bower of our soul blooms.
We are released into the wild of a thousand kisses.
Our home, is a lush island that only you and I can inhabit.
Left alone to our world, we hold each other and
 pray to be together at last in the sunshine.
The world may have the daylight but we will always have the bluest hour,
The dark time when the universe sleeps.
It is then that you can see the passion in our uncaptive

eyes,

A yearning that brings the fountain of our spirit together.

Sack cloth is our daily attire it colors our separation,

But in the night the silk of darkness clothes our souls.

Don't give in to the daylight wait for midnight I shall be there.

We are both just shadows,

The wind waving through the willow tree.

Dusk is like an ornamented   chest that holds the promise of a treasure,

But our whole existence is a dream of daylight kisses.

We have waited a million years for the dawn to arrive,

But our midnight meetings are so profound

 that they can not be replaced by morning light.

Like cats eyes we are accustomed to the dark soft colors of the night.

Tonight like every night we shall be together only shades

 only umbral sprites but that is enough.

Our island rises from tempestuous sea on the wings of music

And we are unchained by the mystery that is our love.

Walls can not contain us, distance can not deter us, our souls stretch across the water,

We can touch with every aural note and

 in that moment the specter of our separation is defeated.

I am here in the midnight moon.

We kiss.

A halo surrounds our bodies.

We have left biology behind, our aether mixes and we

are one.
Our souls are fused by phonons.
Every sprite and faery is our friend.
Together always, always separated.
The dusk and dawn like sand drowns us with hope.
I see the gray shades of your eyes, Your tender smile
The pulse of our hearts heighten.
We embrace like it will be the last time.
Together, caught in the palm of god,
We are free forever at midnight.

PIXIE DUST

Pixie Dust

I once saw the moon sink into the heart of orion.
I once saw a butterfly born from a blacksmith's flame.
Fireflies light the night so that faeries can take flight.
You can not fill a poets pen with credulity alone it will not write.
Pixie dust does not fall like snow it hangs in the air casting a thousand rainbows.
It was a gift from Vulcan to the children of Venus.
Older than Deucalion's flood that wiped the centaurs from ancient Greece so very long ago,

pixie dust, was used on unsuspecting humans.

When a princess falls for a beggar or a King falls for a washwoman these are signs that magic is afoot.

But love is only one of its spells so it is said by olden tales.

It can make the old feel young again and to many it can make a moment much like inspiration.

We can not escape its magic even without or within this nation.

I once saw an old man whose view was colored by the vision of vintage days.

He could only see old age and envied youth in every single way.

He claimed it was far better to be old than to be young.

He had seen comets circumnavigate his lifespan and he once watered a seed in order to see a

great oak tree mature.

He had seen so many things that youth held no allure.

That is the condition the faeries found.

They unleashed the pixie dust.

A thousand rainbows hung in the air.

The old man felt a shiver in his spine.

He looked at the moon he had seen ten thousand times.

It suddenly was new.

The world that was wrapped in winters grasp gave way to spring.

The universe was in bloom.

Phoenix birds took wing.

And there was wonder in everything.

Whatever you believe rebirth is a state of mind.

Whether faeries can renew your flame or whether common inspiration is to blame.

You have to believe that we do not understand all things and neither should we.

Science and magic are of the same source.

They both are explanations for an invisible force.

Science can be beautiful.

But magic can touch our soul.

Faeries found Newton under an apple tree and Einstein starring at the stars.

It is the magic of inspiration that leads to scientific liberation.

When you change the world.

When you see in the ordinary the rare.

Check and see….

You will have pixie dust in your hair.

HAIKU

Haiku

    A moth's wing kissed the sky
    It was not the only kiss
    But the first kiss of spring.

    Winter is my blanket until the flood

Until the rain
Until every stream stretches his hand to the sea.

The cherry is sour. The wind is sweet.
The blossoms like rain.
Every stream has its purpose.
My purpose is to catch blossoms.

Soft like moss.
A butterfly in my hand.
The memory of snowflakes on my lips

I MADE IT HOME

I made it home
I have tasted the apples of Avalon.
Its amazing how a Christmas sky turns from amber
to indigo as
Night closes the eye of day.
The evening star like Aphrodites kiss pierces the
darkness
Then slowly and surely a wide mantle of stars
commands the sky.

I want to go home.

Where Christmas carols brighten the spirit and
warm wasail is served.
The holly on the porch shows its nice noel colors.

My wife is fixing Christmas dinner and she is wearing my favorite dress.
My children are playing in the snow.
The snowman is me.
I come alive as all snowmen do and I chase the children through the yard.
We have a snowball fight and I fall backward into the snow.
We make snow angels as an offering of peace.
I breath in the crisp Christmas air.

I made it home.

The mailman delivers a letter to my wife it reads;
Dear Mrs Johnson we
Regret to inform you that Sargeant Sam Johnson was killed in action today.

I have tasted the apples of Avalon.
Its amazing how a Christmas sky turns from amber to indigo
as the night closes the eye of day.
The evening star like Aphrodites kiss pierces the darkness
Then slowly but surely a wide mantle of stars commands the sky.

I made it home.

(I dedicate this poem to all the warriors of all wars that did not make it home.)

MUSES

Muses

What is a muse?

Like earth drawing inspiration from rain.

Like dough changing into bread by the spirited hand of fire.

Touching our mind like the golden bloom of dawn.

Putting god's majesty in every rose petaled smile.

Sometimes we feel our imagination kindled by a distant star.

Angels kiss us with the breath of spirit.

The seraphic intent is to brighten our minds and put salve on our soul.

While Apollo and Hermes vye for who is the most creative god

It is the nine muses that spark our spirit.

They can fill our minds with a modicum of inspiration

Or fill our souls to the brim with genius.

Sometimes we are like an unchained promethean moth that flies too close to the divine flame.

The muses exact a price for undieng love.

Beethoven who could only describe his muse as his immortal beloved was made deaf to the

Very music that beat so strongly in his soul.

Homer for his poetic vision was left blind to the colors and contours of a world he painted with words.

The ninefold muse is the encourager, the igniter of ideas, the flame that lights every human vision.

Asleep the muse governs our dreams.

Awake the muse directs our mind, moves our pen or paintbrush and fills the world

With art that is her spirit flowing through the prism of our brain.

We do not know her name.

We know her by knowing ourself.

It is her kiss that lights our mind.

We see her reflection in the horizon.

She makes the stars fall from heaven

Perhaps each star is an epiphany.

Perhaps with each thought we are reborn.

REMEMBER

Remember

Remember me when Christmas comes
And the yuletide stars are bright.
Remember me when santa comes
And the reindeer fly in the night.
Remember me when angels sing
And winged seraph's sigh.
Remember me at midnight mass
And when life is holy and high.
Remember me under the mistletoe
And when I steal your kiss.
Remember me in pastoral times
And when life is full of bliss.

Remember me when Christmas comes
And when the starlight calls me home.
Put an empty chair at the feast this eve
And remember though I may be gone
My soul stays near
And I will be there with you
At Christmas every year.

(Dedicated to Leroy Anstead my deceased father.}

POEM TO THE HOMELESS

Poem to the Homeless
Welcome winter.
Steam rises from a street grate.
Red traffic lights presage the season.
Christmas has come and gone in the city.
Today is almost New Year.
Tinsel governs the gala.
I am not invited.
Perhaps next years party will be mine.
But today I live on the streets.
Cold is my companion.
Destitution is my destiny.
Every man in every hour has questioned his faith.
I question humankind.
Will I be kept outside in the dark or invited in?

Do not forget me I once was your brother.
Perhaps love is all I need to rejoin the party.
My simple needs can not compare with your complexity.
If I promise not to stand next to you will you promise to give me shelter?
Don't see me for my outward appearance but for the man inside,
the mirror image of you.
See me with the eyes of god.
Open your heart like a flower
Compassion not wealth is the true power.
If we touch human to human
You will see your reflection in my eyes.
Your smile will be sincere.
You will know there is nothing to fear.

GUARDIAN ANGELS

Guardian Angels
Have you thanked your guardian angel today?
Like lions they roar in the dark.
Stalwart warriors determined to save you
from all circumstance.
They are the watchers, serious sentinels
of every page in the book of life.
Some say they are like the passionate puti
That flocked to aphrodite's aid.

Armed with adoration their cherubic curls
Bloom with lilacs.
They are white winged seraphs not gray
Like god but still mighty in their own right.
Their halo always shines bright. Except when you lie
or are blind to goodness, then the halo darkens
Like an angelic storm that only rests when you
remember to be kind and compassionate.
Their vestment is the silk of heavenly harmonies,
silver and cinnabar in hue, pure as the morning dew.
They play their harps to heal you when you are sick,
and in times of trouble they raise Perseus' shield,
mirrored so that evil might see its own face.
In the palpable loneliness of the soul, when you feel
separated from all who live, your guardian angels
are there so you will know whether away or at home
that you are not alone.

PEACE

Peace
Peace is the polished surface of a lake the mirror of
mankind's highest aspirations.
War is a tempest in a tapestry the image is glory but
the threads are woven from the spirit of sorrow.
We play with our children in the lake of peace.
There is joy for the victors in war but otherwise no

happiness is found.

In the placid lake full of amber dawns there are secret streams that flow into the storm,

for it is what we do with peace that ignites war.

While war itself moves up a river laying waste to all things but no matter what it always

ends in the golden sunset of peace.

We cling to peace never aware of the myriad faults that lead us to war.

The waters are sweet and we never want to leave the lake,

But we become arrogant, impatient and quarrelsome.

We leave the security of peace so that war may swiftly settle our disputes.

It does not.

The question is who will be the better person.

Who will be kind first.

Who will bend enough to make the quarrel end.

We can not make a world on words alone but if we erect the edifice of our actions by just reaching

Out to people, by looking past our differences and accepting the faults of others and by building

The future together.

Then we can hang war's tapestry in a museum. The storm frozen in the ice of the past, aries

Bound up in time.

We will live in the lake of peace building our life in exuberance but still moment by moment.

Forever reaching for the fruit of hope, hesperedian apples that grow in a secret grove and only the

Bravest among us may pick them but always

standing on humanities shoulders.

When we retire from our day at the lake we will visit the museum.

The tapestry hangs like the echo of a nightmare. A tear touches our cheek.

We remember the glory, we remember the sorrow, we light a candle for our friends

For now we finally know that war is gone forevermore.

LEWIS CAROLING

Lewis Caroling

The bundlee comes once a year.

It comes down the chimney screaming all the way.

It is in payment of our griffik ways.

But the bundlee never stays.

It is the bandersnipe not the bundlee that lurks like a shadow at our doorstep.

Its copious drool is hungry for the faltem the very flavor and measure of our soul.

Many persons say faltem is not our soul.

It is the prylick the totemic spirit that is the caretaker of our soul.

The bundlee eats a feast of flesh while the bandersnipe slurps your soul.

The bundlee repays your griffick ways and the the bandersnipe hunts your totemic spirit and strikes like a spider on a fly.

We can not deny the bundlee his prize or the bandersnipe your eyes.

For in those occular orbs is the house of the soul.

But what if the bundlee eats all your flesh what will be left for the bandersnipe?

The bandersnipe will slurp your soul with or without your eyes.

What will you have left over when your flesh and soul are gone?

It is your oona.

That is the seed you plant in every friend.

That is the tree that grows until the very end.

Oona lives in you and I and will be there after we say goodbye.

The bundlee and the bandersnipe can consume us all

but oona will grow its seed and you will remember me.

It may take years and many tears but the garden of oona will grow

And because you believed and were not deceived,

you will become the kind of person that poems were made for

BIOLOGY IS PROFOUND

Biology is profound.
   Life begins with the mother.
   Her body like a hearth warms
   The child.
   Her smile like a rainbow guards
   A treasure.
   Her hands in prayer only ask for
   Her child's joy.
   Peacock feathers were once the
   Eyes of the goddess Hera – who
   Sitting in Olympian splendor
   Watched over the mothers
   Moment by moment.
   My prayers are for my mother
   And I give her this peacock
   Feather so that god might
   Watch over her just as she has
   Watched over me for my whole life. But it is not enough
to let it up to god. For she never let anything
   To god that she could not do herself. So I pledge to do
likewise and do all I can do to bring joy into
   Her life.

From a son to his Mother.

PROMETHEUS' EYE

Prometheus' Eye

I slumber in verdant fields, the rainforest canopy shades me from the stars and galaxies.

Life is concentrated here in the tropics.

Every lightning strike is a neuron firing in Gaea's brain.

Here dreams are the currency of sleep.

Prometheus' eye sees every nuance in a cloud.

Could clouds be our lives?

Could we be living our dream or dreaming our life.

Prometheus promantha is written on my forehead.

Inner sight is the blind poets vocation.

Prometheus means forethought. Could his eye give one advance warning?

I dream of stars in every dream,

I am connected to the flow of living creatures.

Like a billion points of light life beckons my synergy and my synchronicity.

I am open and doves fly from my mind to heaven only

to return as

Couriers of a message "Don't sleep, don't wake, dream awake in the

Pupil of Prometheus' eye."

THE BLOSSOM

The Blossom
The biosphere is blooming.

It is spring and the earth sings lullabys of love.

The planet wears a blue veil in the sunshine   and when she removes it

She has a thousand stars in her hair.

Each animal and plant is a cell in a larger organism,

a great community we call earth.

In the forests and the glade, in the sheer joy of living,

Flowers open their hand to the heavens.

Humanity is but one small branch on the tree of life.

* * *

But each cell competes for supremacy.

What was once a million joyous flowers we leave as a barren landscape.

There is a secret that even the algae knows,

the virtue of each unit benefiting the whole rather than themselves.

The web of life flows through our heart and we are dependant on even the smallest

creatures. To diminish one life diminishes us all.

One day humanity will blossom and when it does kindness and caring will

be the colors of its flowers. We will no longers define ourselves as supreme

but as the engine that makes gaia grow.

The midnight darkness blooms with stars.

Under the twilight moon trees wake up from their dreams.

Spring is swelling with new life. The biosphere is reborn.

By: JF Anstead

EL VELERO DE LA CRUZ

El Velero de la Cruz
   El velero de la cruz
   Su rostro alumbrado por la luz
   Navega las islas benditas
   Las holas saladas y chickitas
   Nunca puede regresar a su patria
   Pero su alma canta con alegria
   Sigiendo la bruhula en las estrellas de la noche
   Velando en la seguridad de su negro coche
   Asta que se enquentra con la luz
   Va el velero de la cruz

SKINS

Skins
   Our skins are the cage for our soul.
   The map of life draws boundaries that seclude us in these skins.

   But God, who opens all cages in the name of love,

   declares the universality of the soul.
               * * *

Love is always the same no matter the gender, color or culture.

Our skins can not block the starlight of our love.

Before we judge others for the love they hold in their hearts.

Know that God does not judge love.

God's expectation is that we love as many living spirits as our heart can hold.

Love is the death of our skins and the birth of our souls.

ODE TO A MASHED POTATO

Ode to a mashed potato
A simple elegant potato when subjected to the magic of milk and butter

metamorphizes into a creamy outcropping of potato cells.

It can be sculpted into devil towers or castle keeps.

It is spooned into a crater and in an act of stunning symbiosis it cleaves to the grateful gravy.

Valleys fill with the dark or light lictor and the sum becomes much

greater than the parts.

There is more philosophy found in mashed potatoes than in the sleepy

gravy symbiont called turkey.

It is not because it tastes better or holds the gravy by greater device.

Mashed potatoes give contrast in three dimensions, pack both

a visual and taste bud punch.

It reminds me to say thank you for all the kindness in my life,

Thank you for the turkey and the family tribe but most of all

for the mash and gravy.

It reminds me that simple things drive our lives

And if you are fair at simplicity don't sweat the

complicated things.

Mashed potatoes are the analogue to life they are good with or without the gravy.

The beauty of living is not in the corn stuffing or cranberry sauce

It is found in the lowly mashed potato because beauty is found in flavours

That warm the heart and save the soul.

In heaven if food is served lo there is a mashed potato.

The everyday aesthetic of the sky, the tree and the butterfly are keen

to the beauty loving eye.

We need no rococo ornaments or Corinthian columns

What we need are the stars served with a slice of the moon.

It is not just bare simplicity that we savour but our connection to heaven and earth.

Beauty is not a contrivance it is the art of the natural.

* * *

Like the beauty of family it is written in our dna

And nobody has to tell us it is beautiful and all beholders agree.

Eat the cranberry sauce, eat the crab stuffing but save the mashed potatoes for me.

SYBILLA

Sybilla
  The vortex in her mind sent shivers down her spine.
  It took twelve secret symbols to decode her incoherent ramblings.
  It was put in neat hexameter by the priests.
  She was the first to chew the laurel leaves.
  First to sit atop the fissure and breath in the generative gases.
  First to touch the stone and evoke apollo's pleasure.
  Aided by the magic of mother earth she would see the fortuitous time
  to plant seed or mate the sheep or bleed the cows.
  War and peace would be engaged on her advice.
  From her name would rises a race of sybills.
  Michaelangelo would paint their fame on the ceiling of the systine chapel.
  They are the origen of religion.

The oracles spoke of a human technology that gave them an advantage over ordinary mortals.

They were the intercessors between god and man.

God spoke to the world through the sybills first.

In the dawn of humanity they were there guiding the shaman under the stars.

Other religions would copy their ability to do great humanitarian works and pray for the multitude.

But they could never capture the essence of true intercessors that through the interaction

With god could make our daily lives better.

She closed her eyes and saw into the mouth of darkness kindled by a vision not of what the

World is but of what the world can be if only we take the appropriate action at the right moment.

THE GATE

The Gate

Do we dare walk through the gate?

Brandenburg like it stands, a stone edifice always there, always beyond our grasp.

Janus like it sits at the threshold, one head looking to the old and another head looking

to the new year. It is all our past failings and all our future ambitions at once.

We may call it December 31st but it should be called the night of hope.

When we begin to dream how tomorrow will be.

When we begin to build the architecture
of our future. Looking with new eyes at our selves
and everything we know.
But will we fail to dream big enough?
January 1ˢᵗ is the only global holiday in existence.
We all use the same calendar and the
change from old to new year is universal. The whole
world honors this one day together
at once. But what should we wish for on the night of
hope?
Before we make resolutions, before we even begin to
dream.
We should think broadly about how our world could
possibly be.
Perhaps we wish for a world without war. Perhaps we
wish for a world where all people
are free. In this dream is a burning ambition that
with persistence, determination and
community can bring about a new day.
New Years day is not just a day to mark our
calendars change. It is a day for all society to come
together.
Not just to celebrate the the arrival of another year,
but to mark the connection between all homo
sapiens, that we are all cut from the same biological
cloth and for one day we are not separated
By borders or the color of our skin or even our
religions, for one day we are unified by our humanity.
The gate will always sit between today and
tomorrow. When the champagne is spent ,when the
Confetti is fallen. You will be there alone with your
wish for the world. Will you truly resolve or like

So many small resolutions will it just be a dream.

The gate is not a building or even a time of the year it is a state of mind.

When we pass through the gate we take up the challenge to put a universal bloom on

The world. It is the time we make our humanity the central player in our lives.

To build a tower of achievement out of our unity, to raise all mankind to higher aspirations,

To believe for once that in our hearts beat the same needs and hopes and dreams and

that we are bound by the genetic sprites that make all of us.

Walk through the gate. The world needs you now.

THE AWAKENING

The Awakening
Sleepers awake.

The universe is not just emptiness punctuated by stars.

We have been asleep.

It is the very source of every ray of life giving light.

To be awake is to have consciousness.

* * *

Drinking nectars from beyond the universe.

Exporting entropy like a living cell.

Symbiotic twins that caprify the stars.

For them galaxies and hurricanes are the same thought.

One mind builds the planet with all its possibility

And the other injects life into the equation.

Invisible snowflakes fall on planetary places.

It is the sum greater than the parts, more than just elements,

Vital essences fertilize matter.

We are the children of the stars.

When you are finally awake you know for certain that you are not alone

And you did not come to be by chance.

There is a purpose for the galaxies,

there is a purpose for you and I.

SPRING

Spring

When Gaia dreams the earth is blessed with spring.

When I dream angelic choruses like a temperate wind blow through the land.

It all begins with a birdsong and grows in harmony to operatic opulence.

In my mind nature has always been my favorite composer.

The simple hum of a bee, the song of cicadas, the startling scream of a seahawk,

nature's music is the manifestation of my spirit.

It speaks in shadow voices, the whispers of spring – full of stories of hardship and pain

that lay a staircase into the upper reaches of my soul.

There I find Butterflies.

God's most splendid ornament, a flying masterpiece that evokes the creators artistic hand.

Butterflies are the stages of the heart:

As an egg they are yet unborn love. A painted mask waiting for its spiritual reflection

to kindle the fire that has always been ready to burn.

As a caterpillar it is earthly passion, erotic arrows and a thousand kisses,

the silk and satin of loves most potent elixir.

As a chrysalis it is all change like a deep water that love explores to unfathomable depths.

We grow closer but all notions of adolescent love are

transformed.

We lay the groundwork in our mutability for the last stage.

The final form is not like the others it no longer needs earthly constraints.

It soars high and feeds on rarefied nectars.

It is the Butterfly – The evocation of True Love.

For Butterflies are the children of spring.

God's name is written on every wing.

Like an artist in love with color spring blooms with blue plumbago, yellow daisies and

rose red tulips.

Flowers are the sentinels of my soul.

When I care to their needs I am not just growing plants but nurturing with every watering

the growth of my soul.

Flowers are the counters of the days.

The river of time flows through each stem, leaf and petal.

Time marches forward and every spring ultimately ends in winter.

Like all true stories seasons move from birth to life to death.

But in the cold end of winter there is the promise of resurrection.

It is in this cycle of renewal that once frozen rivers flow and the skeletons of trees

bloom again with life.

Spring rain is the baptism of the earth and in that beginning our past wrongs are forgiven

if only for just a season.

But if there were no spring the pens of poets would

go silent.

If there were no spring their would be no love and without love god would not exist.

Spring is not just a fashion show for butterflies and flowers.

It is a celebration of life.

How that which you thought was dead came back with full vitality.

It is the secret hidden in every flower.

The road to paradise is built on the edifice of spring.

Once we realize that we can achieve anything.

THE MASK

The Mask
   I wear a red vermillion mask.
   What does it hide?
   Who am I really inside.
   The color of the dead
   Hiding from Hades smile.
   Like Orpheus I wear the mask
   To fool Pluto out of a prize.
   They only see my disguise.
   Not who I am.
   Not the different masks beneath this mask.
   Like layers of an onion
   Hiding Homer and Hercules too

And maybe even hiding someone like you.
All Hallow's Eve is here
So be of good cheer.
It is the season to wear masks.
I am at home in the sea of masks.
Who are we really?
Are we just a disguise?
Does my vermillion vestment fool even the wise.
I will hide behind my mask
Even to the last.
Could I be the ghost of Halloween past.
Tonight I wear my red vermillion mask.
The mask is who I am.
Could ghosts and goblins be who you are.?

My vermillion mask is a red star
Shinning the path home on All Hallow's eve
The most fright
In this dark of night
Is not the monsters outside
It is the question of who are you inside
Are we someone we know
Or do we just pretend to be
Perhaps we are all someone just like me.

CODE OF KINDNESS

Code of Kindness

Napoleon knew what lions know that only the strong survive.

With enough armament life is a breeze of machiavellan ease.

The ways of rough men rule the world and what ceasar says has made the past.

But lost in the labyrinth are the unwritten laws.

A code of kindness that does not define our swords, but defines our souls.

We live such desperate lives but what if instead we could inspire illumination

like the flaming bloom of june.

Perhaps love could kindle that fire and goodness could gain the globe.

Compassion's law is not laid in steel or stone, its foundation is the human heart.

What we must do is draw an arc between each other and make a compact

With all our soul:

Kind people think.

They do not act in a hurry.

They deliberate their destiny and make the universe a wonder to behold.

Kind people care for others.

They use love as their weapon and with warmth they conquer the constellations of man.

Kind people take responsibility,

for themselves first then for all the wide world.

It is possible to make a difference.

It all starts with one flame in the dark, others add their fire to yours and suddenly you have a star.

Kind people cooperate with others.

They leave arguments behind and seek agreement.

For it is in union with others that we can build our bounty, find our fortune, unfold our future.

Let kindness ring a bell of a beautiful new day.

Let it bring sunlight to our soul so we are free to explore our spirit

And sigh to the sky with delight.

HISTORY

History

Some people are content to be keen observers of history. They watch but never become part of the river of actions that make the world. Satisfied to be spectators they never answer the big questions in their heads or make a discovery that takes existence in a new direction. Time has come to turn off the internet to turn off the television. Guide your thoughts by the pulse of your own soul not by the glittering pattern of lights which is a mirage of insubstantial ends. What you should do is reach deep into the hidden continent within your heart. There are yet great things to be done. To dash to the dark side of the moon, to find the occult nexus that will liberate your mind, to be the voice for those unable to speak for themselves. Maybe it is today that you will arm your spirit and challenge the world.   Take a brave step into the future and though you may be afraid you will stride with giants and the crimson in your veins will become the stream of history.

CHRISTMAS ODE

Christmas Ode

Pine trees are emerald islands adrift in a sea of snow.

There are frozen lakes glimmering in the midnight moon.

The entire circumference from cloud to clump of earth is a white wonderland

wrought by the hand of an ice elf.

There is a cavern where the candy canes grow where bubblegum hangs on trees

And toys are not made by machines but by the tender touch of magic.

There is a place of the heart we call home,

where we find our family thinking of midnight memories and the ghosts of ancient noel nights.

Tradition guards the sumptuous celebration.

The lovecrafted food is never the same, though our constant companions are the

cookies, the brownies and the mincemeat tarts.

The serenity is broken by song and gifts that are unwrapped.

It is a silent evening like a snow flake falling in a quiet field.

You feel the charge in the air and the empty corners

of your soul are filled with light.

Perhaps the universe was born on this day.

Whether you believe that Jesus was born in a manger or perhaps that it is

our memory of the beginning when all existence was created.

It is a most Holy day. Heaven lands on earth for one brief moment.

There is a church where all religious roads intersect,

where a single candle in the night evokes the light of our love for humankind.

The Christmas ceremony is joyous and gentle.

Warms hugs are passed around the room. Words of kindness capture our heart.

There is a singular memory of Christmas that I save in my soul,

Where the morning comes and you just know that Santa has arrived.

We all long to be children at this time of year.

to feel the magic, to be raptured by Christmas bells.

It is not just the holly that lives in our hearts but the memory of other noel nights

When we felt the kindness of the universe settle around us and

We could see the goodness of all existence in our neighbors eyes.

Merry Christmas

THE SEVEN VEILS

The Seven Veils

Venus danced slowly like Salome, her face hidden by seven veils.

She was the bride about to reveal her secret.

She was nature uncovering vast wonders.

The first veil is love for humanity.

It is like a gentle rose the flower of our common destiny.

The second veil is love of country.

Like a butterfly it is uncaptive, unchained and free.

The third veil is love of parents.

Like a bear in a cave it is warm, comforting, safe.

The fourth veil is love of siblings.

Like the bird in flight it is joyous and sublime.

The fifth veil is love of friends.

Like sparkling wine it makes us happy down to the last drop.

The sixth veil is romantic love.

Like a mirror it is the reflection of all that is best in you.

The seventh veil is true love.

Like the eternal flame it never runs out of fuel.

With the last veil Venus reveals her face and you realize your resemblance to her.

These seven veils are layers of our soul and when you peel them off you finally understand

That love is not frivolous like fluff it is your inheritance.

Something you can not avoid,
the signature of your heart, the ark of your spirit.

THE UNIVERSE

The Universe
We are made of stardust,

the fertile essence of exploding stars.

Animated by the hidden shadows that spark the darkness.

The music of evolution directs changes   that manifest in our diverse forms.

Like notes of music in a grand symphony nitrogen, carbon and oxygen

Dance a ballet of energy exchanges moving within the atmosphere and also

Through life. Sunlight feeds the tempests and the trees too.

Patterns emerge, from molecules to monkeys, but the fulfillment of life's

Journey is meaning.

Out of the heat left over from creation ,the universe, makes hydrogen.

It binds with itself to create helium and in that deliberate act a star is born.

Hydrogen is the blood of the universe and the act of fusion is the very

Heartbeat of the cosmos.

The soul of the universe breathes and butterflies are born.

We are the stuff of destiny.

Stars organize into communities

And galaxies open like flowers.

I looked at my reflection on the surface of a lake what I saw was an ocean of stars.

The realization was clear I was made in the image of the universe.

THE CHURCH IN THE ATTIC

The Church in the Attic

There is a church in the attic that only the door mouse knows.

All week it is hidden in the dark.

Like if it were a treasure covered by a mist or gold at the elusive region of a rainbows end.

But on Sunday the flame is lit bright.

The people enter the sanctuary.

What was once a utilitarian place becomes a spiritual space.

Caring and kindness soak the air and speakers paint a picture with words.

The ghost of goodness inhabits the assemblage.

The fellowship of friends is like the warmth of winter ages.

The chalice extinguished.

The church vanishes.

It was only visible for a moment.

The door mouse inventory's the hidden hardware.

It will stay in the attic cold or hot but in the daily darkness still a church.

Still the place we gather to fill our soul.

Still where we rest our spirits and sip slowly the peace of the world.

Out of the mist it reappears.

From the rainbows end let us go forth in our faith to the place where our soul belongs.

The church in the attic that like Brigadoon appears once a week

To feed us on spiritual food then vanishes for five days.

It is not just a place where we go.

It is the inspiration that opens our hearts to the world.

It is in the recognition that others like us also care for the universe.

We are not alone our soul has found its home.

(A grateful member of NWCUUC)

TITANIA

Titania
   Pale as morning mist
   She dances in the dark.
   Monarch of mandrake nights,
   Queen of faeries,
   The fluttering lights of midnight moons.
   I wish to kiss her pomegranite lips
   To taste the myrtle on her mouth.
   But beware not too close
   For she will drink
     the dark erythean lictor from your veins.
   Walk with her in the thyme

For just in time
Will you find the garden of your smile.   And not too
late the loving lust of the lake where swan
Apon swan we will father faeries.   Into the wood she
will draw you. You will wander willingly
Lost in her arms your soul will sail the twighlight sea
until titania rests again with thee.

VICTORIANA

Victoriana
   In my rose garden time stands still.
   Golden pools of tea beckon to me.
   Victorian sprites land like ancient lights
   On everything I see.
   Heather grows wild in my mild garden.
   Bee's frolick like faeries round purple berries.
   Censers with plumes of scented smoke
   Rise like the ghost of ancient tombs.
   I have peeled a rind just for me from
   My burnished orange tree.
   The bashful brook by my house is a stygian stream.
   Sail with me like Ulysses into another time.
   When velvet and lace were the common grace
   And every kindness was remembered.
   Through the fog I come awake.
   I am walking by the lip of a lake.
   Swans in a ballet of love swim in sylvan grace.
   The water like silver glows in its serene estate.

Queen Victoria sips Ceylon tea as she looks off
The balcony to the ghost of the sea.
The ocean as a love lost is a whirlpool of emotion.
We see it wash on the shore
But our love is not there anymore.
If the ocean were a flower
It would be a rose in my bower.
Petals playing like a silk maelstrom.
In its turbulence there is utter stillness.
Green fingers fasten over the bulb.
It is the hand of Rhea reaching up from earth
Touching the hidden flower in our hearts.
The stem is covered in thorns,
Aphrodite's armour to protect beauty's virtue
And give passion a chance to bloom.
Dew drops lay on the mouth of the rose.
They are the tears shed by angels
To bring love into the world.
In my rose garden time stands still.
The robin minds her spotted eggs
And though we beg the butterflies are shy.
I will stay here visiting with my ghosts.
The glittering spectre of our beautiful host.
Victoriana.
When velvet and lace were the common grace
And every word was a promise.

THE WORD

The Word

Words are like wandering stars burning with hope and fire.

They are ornaments that affect the mind.

Sustenance for those that are blind.

Words can be noble and divine.

They can declare our independence or restore the rights of mankind.

When manufactured from material kindness they can be the word of god.

Sometimes words are weapons guard wisely what you say for each word leaves its mark.

What we say can bring light to dark.

Words have wings they are zephyred winds that carry knowledge through the loneliness of space.

Words shape existence they have the power for they are the currency of ideas.

If you understand a word it builds the architecture of your consciousness.

But God used one word to bind everything together and set creation in motion and that word was love.

At birth it is the look in every mother's eyes.

And when we die it is the last word caught by the net of our soul.

Give me not ten thousand moments of pleasure but give me one moment of love

And my life is complete.

The strength of every virtue resides in love.

Everyman who has sought truth finds that the only meaning to all existence was love.

If you do not love now then when will you begin.

The job of every celestial angel is to tell humanity, don't' wait love now.

They know all to well that love is not just a word
It is the solution to everyday problems.

So don't wait love now.

MAY THESE WORDS BE LIKE WATER IN YOUR PALM THAT REACHES YOUR LIPS AS A KISS

May
May these words be like water in your palm that reaches your lips as a kiss

May my eyes be like the horizon curled round you and filled with infinite love

May my touch be like the wind that breezes your skin soft as heaven

May my heart reach yours across time and space and nestle close so that it beats forever

Love Joe

ABOUT THE AUTHOR

About Author: JF Anstead

I was born in Enid, Oklahoma, May 2, 1962. Enid is a welsh word made famous by Arthurian legends. It literally means soul. My full name is Joseph Frank Anstead but most people call me Joe.

Because my father was a cartographer I grew up in a series of latin American countries. My very young years I spent in the Andean country of Ecuador. There in the third grade I asked my older sister how to write a poem. My homework assignment made it absolutely necessary. I did not know then that I would be writing poems for the rest of my life.

My late elementary school years I spent in Nicaragua. There we experienced a large natural disaster by way of the 1972 Managua earthquake. While going to school I invented a club called the Spy League of America. It was very successful and the money I made off it lasted me about six years. But it was the friends that I made that I remember most.

My early High School years were spent in Panama, Canal Zone. It was there in the ninth grade that I was published for the first time in the school newspaper. It was the end of an era as soon as we left, the Canal Zone ceased to exist. The world was changing.

My late High School years I spent in Mclean, Virginia a suburb of Washington D.C.. There I took classes at the American Film Institute and later attended George Mason University. I went on to win an award at the Potomac Film festival for a short video about poetry called Le Noir. I also worked a while at an award winning documentary company.

Later I would work for the Defense Information Agency that overlooked all the computer networks for the military. I was an Internet Developer specializing in web animation.

I would go on to design the first 3-D virtual reality shopping mall for a company
named Cybereality

Currently I am Co-Founder of Luxconscientia.com

Now I live in Houston, Texas where I write short stories and poetry for fun and enjoyment.

www.ingramcontent.com/pod-product-compliance
Lightning Source LLC
Chambersburg PA
CBHW071305130626
46556CB00004B/1479

Praise for the books of T. A. Peters

One Little Word

Winner of the Florida Writer's Association's 2016 Royal Palm Literary Award

Official Selection of the 2016 New Apple Book Awards

"*One Little Word* by T.A. Peters is a fascinating tale set in nineteenth century Florida... This is a masterful piece of storytelling, related by an author with extraordinary depth and sensitivity... Mr. Peters has crafted a work of art. His characters come alive in every facet of their development..."

-ReadersFavorite.com

Loggerhead

Winner of the 2015 New Apple Literary Award – Medalist in Historical Fiction

"Peters steeps this yarn in period detail... the narrative moves along briskly, and the scenes are well-staged when jawing turns to fighting. Mary makes for an intriguing heroine: naïve, awkward, mannish, yet entranced by the more assertive Abigail... Readers will find themselves rooting for this Valkyrie as she mounts up for battle. A... rousing saga of a love that dared not yet speak its name."

-Kirkus Reviews

"... a believable and daring lesbian couple... I took almost as much pleasure in their company as they took in each other's."

-Fionna Guillaume, author of
Flowers for the Ancients

Books By T. A. Peters Featuring Mary Fisher

The Green Flourish Pentalogy:

Part 1 - The Sisters Find a New Home

Part 2 - An Unco Body in an Unco Land

Part 3 - La Casa Verde

Part 4 - A First Foot in a Queer World

Part 5 - The Maiden Cruive

Loggerhead

One Little Word

Yet the Sea is Not Full